Poison
Ivy

P o i s o n
I v y

AMY GOLDMAN KOSS

A Deborah Brodie Book

ROARING BROOK PRESS

New Milford, Connecticut

Copyright © 2006 by Amy Goldman Koss

A Deborah Brodie Book
Published by Roaring Brook Press
Roaring Brook Press is a division of Holtzbrinck Publishing Holdings Limited
Partnership
143 West Street, New Milford, Connecticut 06776

Distributed in Canada by H. B. Fenn and Company, Ltd.

Library of Congress Cataloging-in-Publication Data
Koss, Amy Goldman
Poison ivy / Amy Goldman Koss. — 1st ed.
p. cm.
"A Deborah Brodie Book."
Summary: In a government class three popular girls undergo a
mock trial for their ruthless bullying of a classmate.
[1. Bullying--Fiction. 2. Schools--Fiction. 3. Mock trials--Fiction.] I. Title.
PZ7.K8527Poi 2006
[Fic]--dc22   2005017256

ISBN-13: 978-1-59643-118-8
ISBN 1-59643-118-0

1 3 5 7 9 10 8 6 4 2

Roaring Brook Press books are available for special promotions and
premiums. For details, contact:
Director of Special Markets, Holtzbrinck Publishers.

Book design by Patti Ratchford
Printed in the United States of America

First edition May 2006

Many thanks to my big brother, Barry,
for his legal advice.
If any of the law stuff is wrong, blame him.
—A. G. K.

Dr. Sandra K. Horton
Superintendent of Schools
Sea View School District
Sea View, California

Dear Madam Superintendent:

In light of recent events, an investigation
into possible disciplinary action against Ms. Linda
S. Gold was undertaken by the Human Resources
Department. Pursuant to that investigation,
interviews were conducted with several students
in Ms. Gold's classroom. Per your request,
excerpts from those transcripts are attached.

Please don't hesitate to contact me if you have
questions following your review.

Respectfully,

Amy G. Koss

MARCO

I'll tell you what I can, but to be honest, I wasn't paying much attention at first. I half remember Gold wanting to do a mock trial, since we were studying the judicial system and all that. She asked if any of us had any conflicts that we'd like to try in class, but no one did.

She brought it up a few more times but got the same nothing, so I thought that was that. I figured the whole scheme was just Gold's pathetic attempt to wrangle a Teacher of the Year kinda thing or get a raise or whatever. That's what it smelled like to me: a publicity stunt.

But what do I know?

Then the stuff with Ivy and the Anns came up, and it took off from there. It's my guess that Ivy was just looking for a little sympathy. My dad says half the cases clogging the courts are folks who want an apology from people too stubborn to apologize.

But this case wasn't that simple, and it wasn't a very pretty story, so if you're looking for "nice," you better ask someone else. On the other hand, if it's the *truth* you're after, I'll give it a shot.

MONDAY
Cause

IVY

It was the end of the day, so all the fish swam in the same direction: *out* to the breeding grounds. Moving together as the connected scales of one cold, single-minded sea beast. I'd lost track of my binder, however, so I swam upstream, alone against the current. Way off course, like those whales who end up panting in terror, waiting to die on dry sand. Seagulls shriek and circle. Flies appear out of nowhere to swarm. To a whale, flies and gulls are bizarre, nightmarish beings from an alien dimension: *air* creatures!

I felt a tap on my shoulder and assumed, with a spasm of dread, that it was The Evil Three. I pretended I'd mistaken the tap for a stray flick of a passing fish tail. Then a firmer tap and my name spoken in a voice that belonged to none of them. I turned to see tiny Ms. Gold, my American Government teacher, struggling to keep up with me through the mash of fins and gills.

I stopped dead and so did she. The stream of students surged past us. Ms. Gold looked up at me and said, "Ivy, have you got a minute?"

I said, "Sure," although the only thing I was *sure* of was that I'd miss my bus. I could call a cab, but the driver would have to wait while I ran inside to ransack Mom's underwear drawer for money to pay him. Or I could hitchhike home— and probably end up as fertilizer on some psycho pervert's veggie patch, haunting his zucchini.

All Ms. Gold heard was my "sure."

She answered, "Good," and motioned for me to follow her back to the classroom.

When we got there, Ms. Gold sat at Shannon's desk. I

took Bryce Winsky's seat next to her. Then Ms. Gold eased open her notebook, took out a sheet of paper, and slid it over to me.

Oh! How'd she get *that*? Should I act like I didn't recognize it? Run? Say it wasn't mine?

Before I'd settled on a reaction, Ms. Gold said, "Ivy, dear, I find this very distressing. Would you like to talk about it?"

My eye skimmed the page. Not good. The part about wanting to float belly-up. The lines about being spit out by the tide to bleach, beached on the sand, going dry, feeding flies. No, it didn't sound good.

"It's not how it looks," I said.

Ms. Gold nodded.

"It's not like it was a suicide note or anything," I insisted. "I swear! It was more just a poem kind of thing. A joke almost."

She shook her head, not buying it. I noticed that her teeny feet barely grazed the floor.

I could imagine her showing it to my parents. Them blaming each other. They'd reel in the school shrink and who knows how many other "experts." I figured I'd better start treading, and treading *fast*.

"I was so tired of being treated like dirt that I'd just had enough there for a second," I explained.

And that's how it all started. I told Ms. Gold how The Evil Three have been after me, feeding off me since fourth grade. How they'd practically moved inside my skull, making me hear their insults even when they're nowhere around. For instance, they've been calling me "Poison Ivy" for so long that when I refer to myself as just Ivy, it sounds blunt and shortened, even to my own ears. That's how bad it has gotten.

If I were older, I could move away. But for now, I'm stuck with nowhere to turn. I told her all that and more. I told her that Ann was the worst of them, getting right up in my face to sing lead-mean while Benita and Sophie cackled the do-wop backup curse.

I let loose a gush of self-pity—and it felt good. Like finally letting rip with a monumental fart. I told Ms. Gold what The Evil Three did to me on the Catalina Island trip, and I told her about the time they wrote that stuff about me on the board. I rained on and on until I felt light as a cloud and temporarily empty of hate.

Was that weightless, floaty feeling worth what followed? The jury's still out on that one. But Ms. Gold had been itching for a trial, and maybe I always knew that when she went trolling around in the waters, she'd net me.

TUESDAY
Bringing Suit

ANN—The Accused

Can you believe that poisonous little weed? Was I entirely right to hate her guts or what? She must've gone to Ms. G and cried, and told her I'm only the worst person since Osama bin Laden. Benita and Sophie too, but mostly *me*! And now everyone thinks this entire trial thing is such a hoot and I'm all, like, "*What?* Is this even *legal?*"

We were minding our own business when Ms. G nabbed us in the hall before class and said it had *come to her attention*—which meant Ivy told her—that *Benita and me and Sophie have been*—get this—"*emotionally abusing*" a classmate. Ms. G says she has two possible courses of action. One is to report us to Big Bad Broccoli—our illustrious principal, with her *zero* tolerance policy—so we could be suspended, if not expelled, and our war crimes stamped on our records to permanently screw up our lives.

Or, Ms. G said, we could skip Broccoli and do this little trial thing in class. My friends and I would be tried by a jury of our *peers*.

Some choice. I call it blackmail! So I said, "You call that a *choice?*"

And all Ms. G had to say for herself was, "Well, Ann, dear (I *love* the *dear*) you *will* have legal representation to look out for your rights."

And I'm all, like, "*Excuse* me?"

And how were Benita and Sophie about this? Ticked? Pissed? Insulted, like reasonable people would be? Not. Beni was high off the—I don't know what—attention? fame? You wouldn't believe how *giddy* she seemed about the whole stupid—if not out-and-out criminally insane—trial thing.

And Sophie was as paralyzed as if she'd been injected with frozen Botox. A perfect ice sculpture!

I hate to say that my sister was right, but it's true, my gal pals don't exactly burn brightly. Nope, no high beams here.

Anyway, where was I?

Oh yeah. So, the rest of the kids show up for class and Ms. G gives them a pansied-down version of what she'd told me and B and Soph. She tried to make it sound *educational,* since we've been studying the justice system and like that, but it's a feeble ploy. She's just trying to cover up her sicko plot to make me suffer. Ms. G was probably a total gnat in middle school and this is her *revenge!*

Meanwhile, my genius classmates *adore* the idea, of course. What's not to love? They get to burn me and my friends at the stake and watch us scream, while *they* have less than nothing to lose. And all this in front of *Marco,* the only halfway interesting boy in this whole stinking school! Of course this *has* to happen in one of the only two classes I have with him. I guess on the *good* side, if there could be a good side in this mess, which I totally doubt, at least this'll force Marco to notice me.

Did I mention that he's gorgeous? Black hair, blue eyes—my favorite combo. And he's tall but not towering, with glasses that make him look intensely brilliant, and he dresses dark. Not all gelled and studded and *Look how cool I am!* Just plain black. I think he seems older, kind of mysterious, maybe. And he keeps to himself and doesn't run in a pack, although all the guys like him.

I guess you can tell I've got it bad.

Okay, back to the trial. Ms. Gold had everyone (except Beni, Soph, me, and, of course, Poison Ivy) drop their names into a paper bag. Then Ms. G had Beni pull a name to be our *legal representation,* which meant *lawyer.*

I crossed my fingers and silently prayed, *Marco!* imagining me and him having long, steamy late-night meetings, planning our legal strategy.

But does Benita pick Marco? No. Guess whose name she gets instead. *Owen Anderson!* Can you stand it? *Owen* of all people. He's such an egomaniac, thinks he's so hot. And he's not even that cute. We went out for a while last year and it was all about *him!* The live-action, nonstop Owen Anderson show. After maybe five minutes, I'd had enough of that, but he told everyone *he* dumped *me!* As *if!*

Then it's Toxic Poison's turn to reach in and she draws *Daria* for her lawyer. Doesn't that just entirely figure? Daria's only the best student in the class. Actually, I think she got the best marks or scores or something, in all of Sea View not just our weenie grade but Southern California or whatever. That's why everyone calls her "Einstein." She's not exactly personality-plus, but still, brains count for something in the law biz, right?

Then, in case that doesn't reek enough, Ms. G pulls *Jeremy's* name out of the bag to be the *judge!* And the entire class dies.

Especially that dork-wad Wayne Martin. He gets all frazzed and goes, "This total disregard of aptitude or qualifications is absurd! Surely a less arbitrary selection procedure is warranted in a situation like this!" That's how he talks. I guess he thinks *he* should've been the judge, by rights of know-it-all-ness. And for once I practically agree with him, at least for sure compared to Jeremy!

We may as well just shoot ourselves right now because not only is Jeremy a total and complete goat turd, but everyone knows he *hates* Benita ever since she laughed, blowing Pepsi snot-rockets at him, when he asked her out. But to be fair, who could blame her? And now he'll probably give her the death penalty, and me and Sophie along with her!

This is so gross. I hate it here. I hate everyone. I hate Ms. G And I totally hate that infectious Poison Ivy even more than I did before, if that's even humanly possible.

DARIA—Counsel for the Plaintiff

I'm really and truly sorry. I'd like to help you, but even thinking about talking about it makes me queasy. That wasn't my proudest moment; although, I'm not so sure that if I had a chance to do it over, I'd do any better now.

I don't know how to correct the past, the best I can do is attempt to erase it. I doubt I'll convince myself that events went otherwise than precisely as they did, or manage to forget a single moment of the whole horrific ordeal. But I have to try.

I suppose I could save my money in hopes of having my memories surgically erased someday. Would a lobotomy work? Shock treatments? Wasn't there a movie like that?

But even if I could alter my recollection of reality, I could never change the facts. And possibly the worst fact of all is who I am—the precise concoction of phobias and fixations that created the mess that is me, and by extension, made such a dismal disaster of the entire trial.

I'm sorry. Really I am. But you see what talking about it does to me.

MARCO

Gold—that's the teacher—asked who knew the difference between a *civil* trial and a *criminal* trial and not even Wayne Martin raised his hand, which was weird.

"It was thoroughly covered in your text," Gold said with her particularly annoying brand of sarcasm. "The chapters you supposedly read over the weekend?"

Still no hands. So, of course, Gold called on Einstein. And, of course, Einstein knew the answer. That's how she got her name in the first place. I don't know about anyone else, but I could barely hear anything that girl said. Either I'm going deaf or she talks in a range that only dogs, and teachers, can hear.

No matter, I knew I could ask my dad later. He was all over that stuff. He went to law school, even though he didn't end up practicing law. And if he was busy, worse comes to worst, I suppose I could read the chapters.

I don't know why I bothered, but I tried to tell Gold how the Tlingit people use circle talk to settle their arguments instead of suing. But she cut me off, saying, "This is American Government class, Marco. We'll do it the American way."

"Tlingits are Americans," I said, even though I knew she wasn't listening. "They're an Inuit tribe," I added. "Eskimos in Alaska? Alaska, *America*?"

"Take your seat, Marco," Gold demanded, covering her stupidity. I bet she's one of those mainlanders who think Alaska and Hawaii are wannabe states. States clomping around in Daddy's big shoes, playing pretend.

Some teachers prefer their students dumb and smarmy,

kids who'll say *Oh gee! I hope I'm as smart as* you *someday!* Some teachers fawn over the Einstein, Wayne Martin megabrains. Others go for the power-elite—ruling class—popular kids. But so far, there's never been a teacher who likes the kind of kid I am—whatever that is. Not that I care. I'm only stating a fact.

But this one, Ms. Gold, wasn't only indifferent toward me, she hated my guts. I swear I don't know why. My dad says I shouldn't take it personally. He thinks maybe I remind her of a guy who dumped her, or of someone who gave her grief way back. My mom thinks I'm probably imagining the whole thing. But she also says I might as well get used to dealing with different personalities because the world is crawling with freaks.

I considered going to the principal to ask for a schedule change, but Ms. Brock is even crabbier than Gold.

DARIA—aka Einstein

I've given it more thought.

Apparently shock treatments and frontal lobotomies aren't performed routinely on minors in this part of California. And my own efforts haven't made a dent in my nightmares. So, perhaps if you and I discuss it, our conversations will double as low-cost psychotherapy, and help me put the whole unspeakable business behind me.

What I'm trying to say is, I think it's worth a try, if you're still willing.

The beginning . . . Well, starting way back, Ms. Gold wanted to have a trial in class about something real. It could not be a criminal trial, of course, since we supposedly didn't break any actual laws. But a civil trial, meaning between two individuals, as opposed to between an individual and the state. She repeatedly asked the class if there were any conflicts we'd like to resolve, or any differences that needed to be settled. But no one came forth.

It's interesting, on reflection, that I didn't even think of the Ivy situation, and as far as I know, no one else did either. Perhaps we were simply too close to it. On some level, we were all so accustomed to Ivy being mistreated that we didn't even recognize it as wrong.

Therefore, when Ms. Gold announced Ivy as the subject of our trial, I thought, *of course!* It was inexcusable how long she had been enduring torment, and something absolutely should be done to stop her tormentors. Then when Benita, one of Ivy's enemies, drew Owen's name to be the attorney for the defense, I approved even more. Owen was ideal for this—he thrives on attention and he's smart, in his own way.

But when Ivy drew *my* name out of the bag to be her attorney, my insides screamed, *No!*

Ms. Gold chirped, "Congratulations, Daria!" Then, seeing the horror on my face, she added, "You'll do fine, dear." And she rolled on, leaving me breathless with dread. You'll have to ask someone else what happened next, because I was too upset to notice.

I was certain Ms. Gold was aware of my . . . handicap, so I couldn't fathom why she would make me do this. My name had no business being in that bag. If I had no legs, would she have insisted that I dance? Was she insensitive or an outright sadist?

I didn't actually *say* or *do* anything, but panic and anger boiled and heaved inside me. Within the privacy of my skull, I berated Ms. Gold for not asking for volunteers or nominations to take the part of Ivy's attorney. Wayne Martin being the obvious choice. He is obsessed with rules and law, and even totes around a briefcase instead of a backpack. Further, Wayne has a profound natural—or unnatural—distance from normal human interaction, surrounded as he is by a moat of formal icy waters.

There'd been a mix-up at the holy distributor of life events and I'd been mistakenly assigned the role Wayne had been preparing for, in his own peculiar way, all his life. It was crystal clear to me that this error could, should, and must be corrected immediately.

I resolved to march up to Ms. Gold's desk after class, to suggest—*strongly* suggest—that she appoint Wayne Martin to his rightful place as Ivy's attorney—instead of me.

Surely she'd see what a perfect fit he was, and conversely, what a ragged, misshapen misfit I would be in this particular puzzle. Yes! One look at Wayne Martin and it would be settled. Disaster averted, peace restored.

The formulation of that plan allowed me to draw my first full breath of the class period. In fact, it was the only thing that kept me breathing.

Ms. Gold's voice pierced my thoughts when she mentioned something about Ivy and me writing a complaint stating the cause of action. Possibly, if I hadn't felt so close to fainting, I would've remembered what a *cause of action* was, but at the time I had the distinct sensation that a cold steel clamp around my neck was allowing no blood to reach my brain.

I hoped Ivy was paying closer attention than I could at the moment, but one glance at her, plucking fuzz pills off her sweater, squelched that hope.

I forced myself to decode Ms. Gold's words and I eventually understood that she wanted Ivy and me to go sit together *now,* and write down who did what to whom.

I made myself stand and move. It wasn't easy.

I'd never talked to Ivy before. Not even in the most casual, impersonal way. How was I supposed to leap into discussing hurtful things that were said and done to her? How does one initiate something so intimate? It felt wrong. Especially since she'd have to explain it all over again to Wayne Martin as soon as he took over as her attorney.

But for the time being, I was stuck.

You might wonder why I didn't simply raise my hand and voice my objection—speak up and request or demand to be released from my part. Perhaps that would be the recommended action in the manual of mental health, but nonneurotic behavior is not my style. The inability to call attention to myself and my problems is precisely the same inhibition that made the concept of prancing around as Ivy's lawyer so repulsive.

Since it wasn't possible for me to do anything to change my position until after class, I stalled. I took an inordinate amount of time finding my American Government notebook, ever so carefully opening it to a fresh page, and selecting the perfect pen, while Ivy waited in a lump. This did nothing to inspire me to rush to her defense. In fact, each passing moment of lumpishness made the prospect of representing her more and more unpleasant.

As the silence between us grew longer and stringier, I obsessed over the unfairness of it all. Wasn't it bad enough that the kids already called me Einstein? Did I also need to be linked in everyone's mind with Ivy? Poison Ivy and Einstein. Perhaps shortened to simply Poison-Einstein.

Not that I'd ever called her Poison. I'd never called Ivy anything, and had it been left up to me, I probably never would. Not because she was so unpopular, but because there was definitely something off-putting about her.

I know it seems heartless to heap more insults on her, but I also think you should know that, although Ivy didn't deserve the abuse she got from Ann's crowd, she wasn't your typical innocent victim either. Ivy is by no means evil, she simply isn't a particularly likable person.

For one thing, she acts vague. Even when Ann and her friends were torturing her, Ivy seemed not quite *there*. I know it was probably a survival technique—and who could say what I'd do if the popular girls ever decided to rip me to shreds on a daily basis? Nonetheless, at least from the outside, being mistreated didn't appear to devastate Ivy like it would a normal person.

Further, and this is really unfair, but Ivy's voice irritates me no end. It always sounds juicy and gurgley, as if she were drowning in her own phlegm and continually needs to cough or clear her throat.

I know she probably suffered from some awful sinus or throat condition that she absolutely couldn't help. My lack of compassion must seem appalling, and I am ashamed of myself for being so intolerant, but none of that made her voice any less disgusting to me. I hate to say that, but it's true.

And in any case, she *could* help the way she plucked at the front of her sweater constantly, pluck, pluck, with her pointy little fingers. This may be more about my chronic impatience than about Ivy, but I wanted to grab her hands and yell, *Stop that!* I never did, of course. I'm simply telling you that for background so you'll understand that we were not perfect strangers. Obviously, there had already been varying degrees of history between all of us prior to the moment when Ivy and I came to be sitting off to the side of the room, supposedly writing up our *cause of action*.

Ultimately, I asked Ivy what she wanted me to write, and she blinked back at me as if I'd woken her. By the end of the class period, I'd written, *Ann, Benita, and Sophie picked on and humiliated Ivy, calling her names and treating her badly for years.*

I handed it to Ms. Gold, who translated it into this: *Ivy has been the victim of the intentional infliction of emotional distress at the hands of Ann, Sophie, and Benita.*

Then she told the class that Ivy and I had *filed a suit*

with the court. "Now the codefendants have to be served papers," Ms. Gold said. "Which means that the counsel for the defense—that's you, Daria—must give a copy of this document to the process server. Cameron, would you like to be the process server?"

Cameron raised his hand as if Ms. Gold were taking attendance. He has huge hands. Not huge as in misshapen or out of proportion, just huge as in hard-to-ignore.

Ms. Gold went on, "The process server, in turn, serves, or delivers, it to the codefendants, Ann, Sophie, and Benita. Then they must file an answer."

Considering we were together in the same classroom, all that scurrying and copying and delivering seemed fairly senseless. Especially since everybody had to show up for class the next day regardless. But Ms. Gold was determined.

When class finally ended, I marched directly up to her desk, as planned, but so did Ann and her friends. I hadn't factored in that possibility. I went ahead and did my best to insist that Wayne Martin take my place, but Ms. Gold wouldn't hear of it.

"You'll do fine, Daria," she said, with absolutely no regard for my suffering. "Plus, you'll get practice speaking in front of a group. Public speaking is a very valuable skill!"

I wish I'd pressed harder. I know I should have demanded that she take me seriously—insisted that she consider how perfect Wayne was for the part and how imperfect and unwilling I was in comparison. But I couldn't with everyone there, especially since Ms. Gold was so stubbornly ignoring my discomfort.

I'd never hated anyone as much as I hated Ms. Gold at that moment. Unless it was myself.

CAMERON—Process Server

There was so much furniture moving and noise in Government I could barely sleep. It seemed that whatshername and her friends were putting on a skit about getting sued in class for being mean to that girl they're always being mean to. I might'a missed something, but here's one thing I don't get: Why didn't they just apologize? Wouldn't that be way easier than scraping desks around, keeping a guy from his nap?

On my way out the door, the little teacher asked me to be the *process server*. And I thought, *Server?* Like tennis?

But she said, "I'm asking you because of your special skills." And I was still thinking, Huh?

This teacher's just a bitty blond thing, so she looked up at me and said, "Because you're a sprinter!" as if that made some kind of sense.

I was still trying to figure out what track had to do with this court thing. But I nodded and she nodded and we were totally in agreement on *something*.

After practice, I was leaving the gym, all sweaty, when this girl came out of the library and said, "Cameron?" which is my name.

I swear I'd never seen her before in my life, but maybe I had. She seemed to have laryngitis, because she whispered, "You're the process server, aren't you?"

I didn't feel like saying I didn't know squat about it, so I just said, "That's me."

And she slipped an envelope into my hand.

I looked it over. There was no name on it, but it was sealed up tight. "What's this?"

The girl answered but I didn't catch what she said, so I leaned closer and said, "Huh?"

She looked at the floor. I looked at the floor too, in case, but it was just a plain floor. She was trying to speak louder, but her voice was mostly air. She went on talking to her shoes. "You're supposed to hand it to either Ann or Benita or Sophie. It says what they're being charged with. And it tells them when and where the hearing will be held—you know, third hour, American Government, room sixteen."

"Why don't you give it to them?"

The girl took a breath and said, "That's not how it works. I'm Ivy's lawyer."

Which didn't make anything any clearer, but I let it go because she seemed so nervous. I wondered, was it *me* she was so scared of?

I checked the envelope over once more.

"Didn't Ms. Gold talk to you about this?" she asked.

"I just give it to one of those girls? That's it?" I asked.

She smiled, and it made her look a hundred times better. "Yes," she said, "That's it."

"What's it got to do with sprinting?" I asked. "Am I going to have to chase them?"

She laughed a little, as if I were kidding, which I wasn't. Then she turned red and said, "Well, okay then," and she was gone.

Weird kid.

Not two seconds later, Ann and Sophie came out of cheerleading practice. They saw me and said, "Hey," and I said, "Hey" and handed Ann the envelope. She said, "What's this? You having a party?" And Sophie said, "Where's mine?" And I said, "It's for both of you. Benita, too." And they said, "Thanks, Cam!" and I was done.

So what was the big deal?

Ma called me to the phone later and it turned out the big deal was that Ann was so mad she couldn't see straight. All, "Cameron, you *rat*! How could you give me that *thing*? Whose side are you *on*? I thought you were my *friend*," and so on until I hung up with an earache.

ANN

We hopped up there to rage at Ms. G, but our complaints were diddly compared to Einstein's. She was all meek and squeaky, of course, and you had to squint your ears to hear what she said, but in her own Miss Mild way, she seemed *desperate* to get out of this trial. She practically begged Ms. G to swap her for Wayne Martin as Poison Ivy's lawyer. But Ms. G just broomed her outta there, and I totally agree.

I mean, please. What does *Einstein* have at stake? *We're* the ones everyone is giddy to lynch.

Back in class, Ms. G told me and Beni and Soph that we had to write back to Einstein and Poison Ivy saying we either *deny* or *admit* their accusation. But after Einstein crawled off, Ms. G told us that our third option was to say, *"We neither admit nor deny but leave the plaintiff to her proofs,"* so that's what we wrote.

Actually, B did it on her computer that night and made it look entirely legal-eagle, with that olde-Englishey lettering and a swirly, official-looking border.

Anyway, later, Marco was standing right there, being gorgeous, in the hall when Cam gave us that envelope summons thing. Marco didn't say anything and I'm not entirely sure he was even aware of us (which is bad enough), but when we read it and freaked out, I swear Marco *laughed*! When I turned around, he just closed his locker and left. No nod. No smile. No nothing.

And here I'd thought Cam was giving us an invitation to a party, and hoping Marco was invited. I'd wear something deadly and he'd look at me, and I'd look at him, and maybe we'd dance, talk . . . you know.

By the way, it's hard to stay mad at Cameron. I called him and gave him some grief later, but now I'm totally over it. Cam's just an overgrown retriever puppy, cute and sweet and dumb—he probably had no clue what he was doing when he served us those papers.

None of that matters anyway. The *important* question is, Was *Marco* laughing *at* me or *with* me? Or at something else all together?

He sure is one *frustrating* boy!

IVY

During dinner, the phone rang with no one there. My mother, as always, was sure it was my father calling to spy on her. She pounced on it at the first ring and yelled, "Hello, Dumbbell!" into the receiver to prove that she was on to his tricks. That made her giggle proudly till dessert.

I told her I didn't think it was Dad, but she looked at me in that all-knowing way of hers, as if to say she knew better.

I should get kindness points for saying only that I didn't *think* it was Dad, instead of saying I knew he didn't care enough to spy on her.

My mother says stuff all the time like, "I bet your father misses my lasagna." Or, "Your father must wonder what ever happened to my cousin Rhoda."

When she asks me if I told him whatever newsy bits about her life she thinks are interesting, I just say no, which is the truth, although I doubt she believes it.

I act like I refused to discuss her in spite of my father's baited hooks, his wiggling attempts to trick me into revealing my mother's secret info. I let her think I stubbornly refuse to bite, frustrating my father's deep curiosity about her.

Sometimes, though, I'm tempted to let fly with, "Mom, he never asks about you. You're nothing to him." In my fantasies, I often add, "And the only reason he gives *me* the least thought is because he has to."

That might finally shut her up about him. But it definitely wouldn't bring peace. Not the kind of smooth peace that I crave when she jabbers on about him—the peace and silence of a sleek fish in dark water.

My mother says relationships are important. Yet she has no friends or lovers. That's the difference between us. We're both friendless and lonely—but I admit and accept it. And, although I don't like it, I accept that everyone already hates me for whatever mysterious reasons people hate each other. Whether it is my hatefulness or theirs hardly matters in the end.

It occurred to me, however, that this time maybe the hang-up call was someone calling to bug me about the trial. That would be a new level of torture. Until now, The Evil Three never went out of their way to hurt me. They'd never taken the trouble to call. If they saw me, they tortured me, but otherwise I was as free as a fish, alive and unblinking in cool, clean water. It had never occurred to me to be grateful for that!

WEDNESDAY
Jury Selection

MARCO

Gold made us arrange our desks into a courtroom, with chairs in front as the judge's bench, the court reporter's table, and the witness stand. Then two sets of chairs, one as the council table for the plaintiff, meaning Ivy and Einstein, and the other for the defense, Owen and the Anns.

Next, she lined up seven chairs off to the side for the jury. I'd thought there were always twelve people on a jury, but it turns out you can cut it in half for a civil trial. And it's seven, instead of six, in case someone flakes.

To find the lucky seven, Owen and Einstein (the two lawyers) were going to ask each kid in class a bunch of questions. The idea was that both lawyers had to agree on all seven jurors. Gold said each lawyer could refuse six kids, max. That sounded like it would take forever, and since I sit near the back of the room, I figured they'd have suckered in all the jurors they needed long before they got to me.

I sat back to enjoy the show.

It started with Jeremy-the-judge hauling out a hammer from home and preparing to whack his desk into splinters.

Gold got it away from him. "Judge's gavels are made of wood and are mostly symbolic," she said. Jeremy grumbled but pulled himself together enough to let the jury selection begin—in its own zoolike way. First, he told Bryce (who sits in the front row closest to the door) to state his full name.

"Dude, you know my name," Bryce said, cracking everybody up, except Jeremy, who snapped, "I order you to state your full name or suffer the consequences!"

Gold, playing the bailiff, but without a gun, told Bryce to answer the question or be held in contempt of court.

"Meaning I'd flunk, or what?" Bryce asked.

"Meaning you should state your name."

So Bryce did.

Then Gold called Einstein up. She didn't call her Einstein, of course. She called her Daria. I don't know when Einstein got named "Einstein." And I'm not all that sure why she was called that, either. She's a good student gradeswise, but she's way too quiet to *talk* smart. She always has her nose in a book, for what that's worth, but still, if anyone was going to be dubbed "Einstein," you'd think it would've been Wayne Martin.

Anyhow, Einstein was supposed to be Ivy's lawyer, which was just plain ridiculous. Einstein was so shy it hurt to look at her. You knew this lawyer thing must've been murder for her.

I wished she'd lighten up for all our sakes, but I wasn't holding my breath. I read once—in my dentist's waiting room—that shyness isn't just a personality thing. Sometimes it's genetic. It said there were even shy babies, and you could tell by how they reacted to new stuff in their cribs. Einstein was clearly one of those who'd been scared stiff by the sight of her rattle. It must be a huge drag to be her.

Anyhow, when Gold called on her, we all had to watch Einstein get up and walk in total misery over to Bryce. Then she asked him something no one could hear.

Jeremy banged his desk, making her cower even worse.

"Speak up!" Jeremy yelled. "No secrets in the court!"

Einstein locked her arms as if she thought someone was going to punch her. Then, in her tiny flea-voice, she said, "I have no further questions."

"No further questions, *who*?" Jeremy bellowed. "You're

supposed to say, 'No further questions, *your honor*!' I demand to be called *your honor*!" Everybody ignored him. Jeremy sulked.

"Daria, dear," Gold said. "You need to be a bit more proactive in selecting this jury." But too late—Einstein was back in her seat and clinging to it as if it were a life raft. It looked like Gold would have to pry Einstein's fingers loose and drag her out of that seat if she wanted her to get up again. Instead, Gold called Owen, the attorney for the Anns.

Everybody knows about Owen and Bryce. They used to be best pals, but now they hate each other.

There was a fight. If I've got it right, it started out as just normal killing-time-after-school, waiting-for-the-bus stuff. Owen grabbed Bryce's Dodgers cap, tossed it to someone, playing pickle, messing around. But you've seen Bryce, right? He's a short guy, so maybe a little extra touchy. And there he was, having to jump for his hat. Trying not to act pissed, and all kinds of girls watching. It wasn't funny anymore, but Owen wouldn't let up. Waving Bryce's hat out of reach, catching it behind his back, laughing.

So, finally, enough is enough, and Bryce hauls off and decks Owen dead-on.

Owen's nose explodes. Blood gushes all over the place. He completely freaks and starts kicking Bryce, *bam, bam,* in the shins. Calling him "mutant shrimp," "micro-midget," "pin-dick," like that, fighting dirty. Way uglier than necessary. They had to be pulled apart by the bus drivers, and they never patched up.

Now there's Bryce on the witness stand with Owen pacing in front of him, playing lawyer.

First question out of Owen's mouth was to ask Bryce if he'd ever been picked on. I don't know how many other kids in the class flashed back to that fight, but I did.

Bryce answered with a shrug.

Judge Jeremy growled, "I order you to answer *out loud*! *No* shrugging!"

Bryce rolled his eyes at Jeremy, then said, "What was the question, dude?"

"Have you ever been picked on?" Owen repeated.

Bryce said, "I guess."

"Yes or no!" Jeremy yelled, taking his judgeship over the top.

"Yes!" Bryce yelled back.

Owen nodded and asked, "Have you ever bullied anyone else?"

"I dunno," Bryce answered. "Maybe in a way, dude. But just screwing around."

Owen nodded again. "And do you think Ann, Benita, and Sophie intentionally caused Ivy emotional distress?"

Bryce said, "Dude?"

Owen pointed to the Anns with their desks pushed together and said, "Do you think they're guilty of bullying Ivy?"

"Well, du-uh," Bryce said. "They only, like, pick on her constantly, dude. Everybody knows that."

"Objection, you nit!" Ann called out. "We're supposed to have a *trial* first! Before you talk about *guilt!*"

Benita giggled. Sophie sat there looking stoned.

"Ann, you can't object to anything right now," Ms. Gold told her. "And it's your attorney's job to do the objecting."

"But our so-called *attorney* is letting Bryce talk trash about us!" Ann said, glaring.

Now Benita's giggles became the crazed kind that probably hurt her face. I wondered if she'd pee her jeans.

Owen turned his back on Ann and nodded to Bryce. "As you were saying . . ."

Bryce grinned even wider. "Just that every fool in this freakin' school knows Ann and them are low-down and nasty as rabid dogs. If they weren't chicks, all three would'a had their teeth kicked down their throats by now."

"*What!*" Ann shrieked.

Bryce shrugged. "The truth hurts, but I'm under oath!"

Ann gave Owen a shove. "*Excuse* me, bud!" she barked. "Are you forgetting which side you're supposed to be defending?"

Owen said, "Listen, Annie, it's not *my* fault if everyone knows you're guilty!"

Ann went ballistic. "Hey! Is he allowed to say that?"

"Owen, Ann," Gold said, "that's enough, you two." Then she nodded at Jeremy, who took his cue to start yelling, "Order in the court! I demand order in the court!" Ann raised her voice over his to scream, "What happened to *innocent until proven guilty*? What happened to a *fair trial*? Isn't this *America*?"

Owen calmly studied his fingernails until everybody quieted down. Then, as sarcastically as possible, he said, "Very well then, out of deep respect for Annie's honorable feelings for truth, justice, and the American way, I refuse Bryce from the jury." Owen bowed smugly left, right, and center, as if to wild applause, then sat down.

Ann steamed. Hard to believe those two, her and Owen, used to be so hot for each other that the lunch room was practically X-rated when they were together.

Gold told Bryce he was dismissed.

"Dude! You mean I can leave?" Bryce asked hopefully, pointing to the door.

"No, I mean you can step down," Gold said.

"Down?"

"It's an expression," Gold explained. "In a real courtroom, the witness stand is raised, so you'd have to step down to leave it. Witness *stand*, jury *box*, judge's *bench*. We have to use our imaginations." And she smiled.

If I'd called Gold "dude" or said half the things Bryce did, I'd be on my way to Principal Brock's office. Not that I want her smiling at me, I'm only saying we are not all equal under the law.

Anyhow, she asked him if he'd like to be the court reporter, and Bryce shrugged.

Jeremy slammed his desk. "I said no shrugging! The next shrug walks the plank!"

Bryce gave Jeremy the finger behind his back, while telling Gold he couldn't type or write fast or anything.

"Can you run a tape recorder?" she asked.

Bryce shrugged once more and Jeremy leapt to his feet, fists in the air. "That's it!" he hollered, but no one paid any attention.

Gold made Shannon stand up next. Do you know her? She's the one who tried to pierce her own belly button as her demonstration in speech class. No joke. She got an ice cube and brought in a needle and, man, it was intense! But anyhow, Shannon sits next to Bryce, so she was next.

Jeremy told her to state her full name.

"What do you mean, *full*?" Shannon asked.

Jeremy said, "Full means *full*!"

Shannon stuck out her chin and said, "My middle name doesn't have anything to do with this."

Jeremy insisted that the law was the law.

Shannon still refused.

They went back and forth until Jeremy threatened to tear Shannon's middle name out of her with his bare hands. And Shannon hissed, "Or die trying."

Gold, probably picturing the bloody scene, settled it by saying a middle initial would do.

Shannon admitted her middle name began with *M*.

Einstein scraped together a voice and asked Shannon a few questions that I missed, partly because I was trying to figure out what Shannon's *M* was for. *Mistake? Moron?* But mostly because Daria's volume control was stuck on mute. Not that it mattered, though, because all Shannon did was lie through her braces, saying she'd never heard or seen anyone being mean to Ivy.

Gold had said this jury selection process was called *voir dire,* which was French for "to speak the truth." Ha! The truth obviously had nothing to do with this case.

Shannon opened her eyes as wide as humanly possible, in what she must've thought was an expression of Bambi-esque innocence and insisted she could be totally fair and impartial and would make an excellent member of the jury.

I half expected Einstein to either pass out or dematerialize completely into vapors, but she managed to stay standing and whisper to Gold that she didn't have any more questions.

Jeremy couldn't take it. He hauled off and pounded his desk with his bare hand so hard I heard a crack. "Einstein!"

Jeremy yelled. "Don't be crazy! You don't have to put Shannon on the jury!"

Then other kids called out, telling Einstein to dump Shannon while the dumping was good. I remember Bryce shouting, "Dude! That chick be some *evil* nasty!" But Einstein didn't refuse Shannon for the jury. And she didn't refuse anyone else, either. I'm not sure what Einstein was thinking, but my guess is that she didn't want to get involved—even though she already was. Like the bystanders who stand around with their thumbs up their ass while some poor jerk gets attacked and murdered right in front of them. And they don't call the cops or run for help or whatever. Like that. Does that make any sense?

Anyhow, I don't know what the other kids are telling you, but as far as I'm concerned, Shannon would've turned in her own granny in a heartbeat if it meant she could sit at the lunch table with the Anns. Heck, Shannon would turn Granny in just to be allowed to sniff Ann's shoes.

There wasn't a doubt in my mind how Shannon M. would vote on that jury, meaning the whole thing was a total joke—and it hadn't even started yet. But so be it; the fix was in. Shannon became Juror Number One.

IVY

How does every fish in a silvery school know to turn with the others the way it does? They're swimming one way, then flip, they're going the other. Maybe it just *looks* like they do it all at once. Maybe if we played it in slow motion, we'd see that some hesitate, others anticipate. Some lead. Some swim so close to the fish in front of them that they don't even realize they're turning. Maybe they just get swept along. But swept along like, *Whee! Great ride!* or swept along like, *Help*? Maybe it's the same either way.

I never knew Shannon hated me. I'd never thought about her one way or another. Just one more flickering flash darting past, with minimal brain activity and cold blood.

DARIA

By the time class was over, my throat hurt, as if I'd swallowed ground glass and my skin felt seared from being looked at. This may sound insane, but until then, I'd basically believed myself to be invisible. What I mean is that, usually, if I remain still, my natural camouflage kicks in and I more or less blend safely into the background. But this trial tore off my protective coloring and shoved me into the bright lights of everyone's scrutiny.

Ms. Gold hadn't said how long this ordeal would last, but we'd picked only three jurors and we couldn't even begin the trial until we had six. Seven, actually, counting the alternate.

I tried reminding myself that this was a good thing. It was Ivy's revenge after all those years of pain. But as mean as Ann, Benita, and Sophie were, letting people like Bryce get up and call them names for calling Ivy names didn't seem right either. Wasn't that a little too eye-for-an-eye for American Government? I thought we stood for something other than simply moving the same hunk of cruelty around from victim to victim. The whole thing gave me a crushing headache.

Jeremy caught me right after class and said, "If you refer to me as 'Your Honor,' I'll pay you, I swear."

I have no idea if he was kidding.

Then he said, "And I definitely think it'll feel more realistic if everyone stands up when I enter the room, don't you? You know," he continued, making his voice low, "like, 'All rise! The honorable Judge Jeremy presiding'?"

I didn't respond.

Wayne Martin stopped me next and asked if I thought justice was being served. I knew Wayne well enough to know that he was not joking. Wayne is entirely humorless. You might wonder who *I* am to talk about being fun-impaired, seeing as I'm not exactly a party girl, but with Wayne it's something else. He's *stern*. I know that's usually a word for an elderly piano teacher who scowls when you hit a sour note, but in Wayne's case, it fits. It is more about his being exacting than mean, although the feeling it inspires is identical.

I speak from years of unwanted experience. Wayne and I have been forced together since first grade. When we were younger, it was spelling bees, math competitions, and geography challenges. It continues with test scores, national standing, and awards. The only escape from being continually teamed with or pitted against Wayne Martin would be to intentionally fail. As tempting as it is to be free of him, he isn't worth sacrificing my future for. I may be crazy, but I'm no fool.

Was justice being served? What a question. How was I supposed to answer that? It felt more like my heart and lungs were being served—on a platter for the whole class to devour.

But Wayne didn't wait for my answer to his unanswerable question. He went on to say, "I trust that you appreciate the gravity of the authority entrusted to you. That of defending Ivy's right to her own pursuit of happiness, unimpeded by the viciousness of a few sick individuals."

I had no answer there, either, but it didn't matter—Wayne wasn't finished. "When confronted with a situation of such profound constitutional implications," he said, "threatening the very foundation of our American way of life—our basic inalienable right to live free from persecution, as Ivy has certainly been persecuted—one must reach deep into one's core for the strength and courage to meet the challenge!"

Then he nodded, satisfied with himself.

"I'd be more than glad to ask Ms. Gold to give *you* my part," I offered. "In fact, I already tried once."

But Wayne shook his head. "No, no, the decision, no matter how arbitrarily, has been made. But I have every faith that good will triumph over evil. And those who acted with blatant disregard for human dignity will be brought to understand the profound error of their ways."

He seemed done, so I said, "Thanks?"

He nodded and scurried off, reminding me, as always, of a muskrat.

I had PE next and I felt more exposed than ever in the locker room. This trial had focused a merciless light on me, which seemed to magnify my every pimple and pore. While I was changing into my gym clothes, I apparently came into focus for several girls who'd never spoken to me before. One of them, a girl named Jennifer, who dresses like a Halloween witch, suggested that I request various body parts as payment from Ann and her friends when they were found guilty. Eyes, lungs, livers, ears.

All I could think of was that if I'd known I was going to lose my invisibility, I wouldn't have worn this ratty old bra.

ANN

Later, Beni goes, "I can't believe we're stuck with Owen as our lawyer! Ick! He's such an idiotic idiot. No offense, Annie."

"Meaning what, may I ask?" I ask, although I knew she meant my going out with him for three seconds last year. Like Beni never in her whole life had a flash of *stupids*? Please.

Benita gives a half shrug.

Meanwhile, Soph says, "What I can't believe is that I'm even *part* of this! I've never said a single thing to Poison Ivy and you know it. If you were *real* friends you'd explain that to Ms. Gold, and get me off the hook!"

Beni and I stare at her with our jaws entirely on the floor.

So then, in an even whinier voice, Sophie says, "What? You know I'm right! You both totally know I'm being blamed just because I'm friends with you. I've always been the nice one! I've never spoken a mean word to Poi—, I mean *Ivy*, in my entire life."

We're still sag-mouthed.

"Stop looking at me like that!" Sophie said. "It's true!"

Beni finally went, "That is such a load, Soph. I cannot even begin to believe you're even saying that."

I cracked up a little about Sophie going from frozen solid over this yesterday to all hot and hairy today.

Soph stomped her foot. I looked around hoping no one was going to witness her little tantrum. "It's true," she insisted. "I'm totally, totally innocent! And you know it! I'm just getting blamed because I hang around with you two!"

I thought, We can solve that easily enough. And say, "You don't want to hang with us? Fine!" And I grab Benita and start to walk away.

Then Sophie calls out, "My mom was so totally right about you, Ann!"

That was meant to cut deep, but *please*. Sophie's mom always blames everyone but her precious angel. Back when Soph got caught smoking in her garage—oops! I *swore* I'd never tell—her mom entirely bought Sophie's lie that they were *my* cigarettes and I'd *dared* her to try one!

Anyway, I took my seat next to Marco in science. He was listening to the Ramones. I could hear the bass notes through his headphones. He didn't even nod at me. So much for my new black jeans.

Everything stinks. This trial thing is so *foul,* and now Soph is acting like such a *traitor* and Marco is oblivious, and just everything is a bowl of puke.

MARCO—Juror

Out of nowhere, Ann Martello stopped me. I took off my earphones and said, "What?"

"I asked you about the stuff you were telling Ms. G about Eskimos yesterday?" she said.

Ann is the last person I'd expect to be interested in . . . well, in anything, so it took me a full beat to get my bearings. Meanwhile, she said, "You know, like you were saying how in Alaska they've got another way to sue people or whatever?"

I was dumbfounded, half by the disconnect of an Ann talking about something besides lip gloss, and half, I hate to admit it, by how incredibly hot she was. In spite of knowing her to be a total jerk, I was blown away by her looks. Finally, I said, "You're asking me about the Tlingit?"

She smiled and said, "*Brilliant,* Holmes!" in a teasing way, like we were pals.

I noticed that her skin doesn't look like it's made out of the same stuff as other people's skin. It's very distracting skin. Hard not to wonder if it's that smooth everywhere.

But I made myself concentrate on explaining how the Tlingit elders gather together everybody who'd been affected by a crime, like the guy who had his dogsled stolen and the guy who stole it and anyone else who was involved, like maybe the guy who'd been waiting for his dogsled delivery, and they all sit in a circle.

Somehow we'd left class together and were walking down the hall at this point, and even though Ann kept saying "Uh-huh" and "Go on" as if she were listening, I saw her wave and nod at people we passed, like royalty on parade. I bet everybody wondered what Queen Ann was doing with someone as profoundly nerdful and geekish as myself.

I heard my voice grinding on and on, explaining to Ann that the Tlingit use a talking stick, or a talking object, and no one can speak unless they are the one holding it. "No one can interrupt anyone else. One person talks at a time, and when they've said everything they want to say on the subject, they pass the talking stick to the next person. It never goes out of order and no one gets a second chance to talk until everyone has had their first chance."

"So you think we should all sit in a circle?" Ann asked me.

"It works for them," I said lamely.

"Well, but they're, like, *primitive*, right?" she asked.

"We send crooks to jail," I explained. "That might protect other people from getting robbed, but it doesn't do much to help the poor guy who has already been hurt. His lawyer speaks for him, in his own lawyer way, but the victim himself never really gets heard. He never gets to say, 'That wasn't just any old thing you stole, it was the sacred, ancestral thing, handed down through the ages and left to me by my great-grandfather on his death bed.' They figure that if the thief understood how awful he'd made the victim feel, he'd be so sorry that he'd do whatever he could to make amends."

It occurred to me, at the distant outer reaches of my consciousness, that the beautiful girl so close beside me was, in this case, the perpetrator who didn't care how her victim suffered. Ann didn't seem to recognize herself as the villain, though. And she sure didn't look evil, with that skin, those big eyes . . .

"I had no idea you were so *sensitive!*" she said. "I wish you were *my* lawyer!" Then she tugged my sleeve in a playful way that probably didn't mean a thing, but my arm instantly burned where she'd touched it.

Forget hydrogen cars and hybrids and oil wars. If engineers could harness the power of a sexy girl, there'd be no fuel shortage. And I don't even like Ann. I know she's an airhead. I know she's a bully. I know she couldn't care less about the Tlingit or anything else. I had no idea why she was messing with my mind, but *phew!* Being close to her, and touched by her, well, what can I say? It was both the best thing that ever happened to me and like being hypnotized and made to squawk like a chicken.

It wasn't until she'd disappeared through a classroom door that I realized I'd walked her to her class and was now late and at the farthest possible end of campus from where I needed to be.

Squawk!

IVY

Sophie swam up to my locker between classes, and my first reaction was to duck. But she didn't slug me. She said, "Can I talk to you for a sec?"

I was tempted to tell her to speak to my lawyer, like they say on TV, but I didn't.

An essential part of The Evil Three phenomenon was that it worked only in groups of two or more. Tormenting me was a spectator sport, performance art. Without each other as audience, I wasn't worth their individual effort. I knew this because when any one of them chanced upon me alone—turned a corner in an empty hall, or ran into me in the bathroom when no one else was there—they'd develop an instant blind spot for me. I'd become as invisible as a ghost.

Not that it happened very often. In fact, I can probably count each of the times I found myself alone with any of them. But every rule has its exception, like the time with Ann way back, on the sixth-grade camping retreat on Catalina.

The days weren't so bad there. But in the cabins at night, there were no park rangers or camp counselors, and The Evil Three were out for blood. Maybe they were homesick or scared of the dark and the only comfort they could find was being extra nonstop horrible to me. Or maybe they'd just never had the chance to go after me at night before. I don't pretend to understand what fun they got out of tormenting me, but whatever it was, those nights on Catalina were the worst.

Then the last night, the naturalists took us snorkeling,

and it was amazing. Floating facedown in the ink-black water under the ink-black sky. No sound but my own breath bubbling up through my snorkel and the most incredible view of the watery world lit by the beam of the headlamp strapped to my forehead. The kelp swaying beneath me, like the very top of Jack's beanstalk, the sea floor thirty or forty feet below.

It wasn't about color. The fish were mostly brownish and mud-colored. Even the seaweed was a grayish-greenish brown. Maybe that was the muck and pollution from shore, maybe it was camouflage, but it sure wasn't the glam bright-striped and polka-dotted marine life you see in photos. I guess I'd expected it to be like the crystal-clear aquarium in my doctor's office, only bigger. But it wasn't. It was gorgeous and real.

All the pieces were interrelated, moving with the tug of the surf, as if dancing together. Nothing slammed or lurched down there. There was nothing abrupt or harsh. Just smooth, graceful movement. I wasn't disappointed at all by the lack of color. It seemed perfect.

Then, in silence and without warning, the water came alive, filled completely with swarming motion! I was surrounded by countless flickering fish bodies, brushing against me. For that split few seconds, or whatever magical timeless period it was, I can honestly say I was happy and nothing hurt. I was absolutely one of them and not even remotely alone.

Then, all in a blink, the fish were gone.

I lifted my head to laugh or cheer over what had just happened. And there, laughing and gulping air not three feet from me, was Ann, with her headlight bobbing crazily.

She looked right at me and shrieked, "God! That was awesome!" We grabbed hands in the excitement, and I remember yelling, "Wow! That was so incredible!" We both sputtered and hooted and kept saying things like "Can you believe how *many* there were?" And "Did you *ever* see anything like *that*?" And "What *were* those fish?"

After we'd caught our breath and the moment of sheer thrill faded, we put our masks on, lowered our faces back into the water, and swam our separate ways.

Needless to say, neither of us ever said anything about that time, and who knows, maybe Ann forgot all about it.

But you can see why having Sophie approach me at my locker, all by her scrawny self, and speak to me as if I were actually there, was rare and, well, interesting. Curiosity, if nothing else, kept me rooted to the spot.

She smelled like cigarettes and Altoids, and she was wearing this really greasy red lipstick that she must've put on without a mirror. It missed her lip on one side and went halfway to her nose. So even if she wasn't curling her lip in a sneer, it sure looked like she was.

I watched her mouth as she spoke.

She asked me if I'd ever in my life seen her be mean to me, and I thought, "Only every day since I was, like, nine." But I didn't answer. I kept my face blank as a fish's, thinking, Nose, stay bland. Forehead, bland. Eyebrows, lips, chin, cheeks, bland, blank, as empty and expressionless as death. My emptiness made Sophie twitch.

Then, with her twitching, sneering face looming like the blimp, Sophie said, "I mean, really, think back. Do you remember ever specifically seeing *me* be mean?"

I held tight to my frozen blankness and did not scream,

"Of course I've seen you be mean! I've never seen you be anything *but* mean."

She was getting plenty annoyed. "It's just that I think you're mistaking me for Benita and Ann," she whined. "I think you're lumping us together and that's totally not fair!"

How bizarre! Sophie was talking to *me* about fair! I smiled from ear to ear on the inside, but kept my face a wooden mask.

"I'm serious!" Sophie insisted.

I closed my locker and spun the lock. Then I walked away. I may have hunched my shoulders and turtled my neck, half expecting Sophie to heave her heaviest textbook at the back of my skull. But even if she had, it would've been worth it, just knowing I'd left her gaping like a fish.

MARCO

Ann.

For a minute, walking down that hall, I'd believed she actually *liked* me, which was weirdly flattering, even though she's a jerk. I remember seeing her wrapped around Owen last year. Her hands in his back pockets. His fingers all tangled in her hair. Hmm, I guess I'd watched more closely than I realized. Stared, is probably more like it. Drooled.

Now it was *me* she was asking questions, acting interested in. She was matching her stride to mine, with her little shoes, her amazing legs.

Or had I matched mine to hers? I'd probably lumbered clumsily along, yammering away about the Tlingit, long after she'd lost interest. Had I waddled earnestly, oafishly out of breath? Or scurried beside her, tipped eagerly forward, obsessively shoving my glasses up my nose in a nerdish frenzy?

She couldn't have been interested in *me*, so for a second, I thought maybe she was interested in the Tlingit tribesmen. But that made no sense. In my own defense, I should explain that I was Ann-blinded, which is a lot like snow blindness, which stuns you stupid. Ask any guy who has seen her, and they'd totally get it.

Eventually, one fact cut through like a warm knife through butter: Ann was probably making sure I was on her side, in case I got on the jury. Was she going through the whole class, casting spells, messing with minds? I wondered if it would work as well on the girls.

I felt like such a dork for letting her lead me around like that. The image of myself following her to her class, tail wagging, tongue lolling, ranting about Eskimos, made me cringe. She must've laughed her head off over how easily I fell.

And she was in my science class, too. Sat right next to me. I wanted to ditch, but then what? What about tomorrow? Ditch the rest of the year because I let Ann make a fool of me?

It was tempting.

I kept my headphones on instead and stuck my beak in a 'zine. Man, that was one long class. One l-o-n-g day.

When I finally dragged my sorry self home, my mom reached for my forehead. "You feel okay, Marco?"

"Rotten day," I explained, ducking her concern and heading for my room. I figured any sympathy and I'd probably bust out crying like a baby. That was way, way more power than I wanted a witch like Ann to have over me.

Nonetheless, in spite of all my intentions to rid my mind of her, Ann snuck into my dreams that night in a big way.

THURSDAY
Jury Selection
Continues

ANN

Owen's such a turd. There he was, in my first-period homeroom, doodling on his skinny arm with a Bic. So I go up to
him and say, "Let's work on my case."

And he goes, "I'm busy."

I look at the stupid dragon he's fake-tattooing, and I go,
"Yeah, right." Then I say, "On TV they're constantly plotting
and planning and looking for witnesses and all that."

And he has the nerve to say, "Sure, Ann. Like there's
really someone out there who'd be *your* witness."

And I go, "*Excuse* me?"

So he rolls his eyes and says, "You picked on Poison Ivy
all the time, in front of everyone, and you got caught. You
lose."

How *dare* he? I thought. "How dare you?" I asked.
"Don't you know that in America, the lawyer's job is to
defend a person's innocence?"

"You don't have any innocence to defend."

"You're fired, you butthead!" I yelled. "You are so
entirely *fired*!"

"Fine," he answered. And went back to his stupid dragon. Can you believe him? Can you believe what an un-
American turd he is?

I was so totally right to dump him last year. That's
probably the rightest thing I've ever done in my life. Not
that I ever doubted it for a split second.

And you know what? Back when I wanted to end it
with Owen, I told this kid, Bryce, do you know him? Short
guy? Always wears a Dodgers cap? Well, Bryce and Owen
were best friends back then, so I asked Bryce to tell Owen

that I didn't want to go out with him anymore. I figured Owen would *rather* hear it from his bud than from me, and I was being *nice*.

But you know that thing about blaming the messenger? How kings used to kill the poor fool who *brought* them bad news, as if it were his fault? Well, when Bryce told Owen I was breaking it off, Owen went totally psycho, calling Bryce names and starting an old-fashioned fistfight with him!

How's that for an attack of profound, incurable *weirdness*? And, if *that's* how he took one measly breakup, you can totally imagine how much I *don't* want his flaky "help" in this trial. *Right?*

I tracked Beni down after homeroom and told her I'd fired Owen's pimply butt, and good riddance.

But she got all panicky, with her eyes darting back and forth. "He was *my* lawyer, too, Annie!" she whined. "Now what am *I* supposed to do?"

I reminded her that we were in this *together* and that if Ms. G won't assign us a new lawyer, we could be our own lawyers.

"But what about witnesses and stuff?" she asked, blotching all of a sudden like she was going to cry. "And now that Soph is worming out of it . . ."

"She *can't* worm out of it," I reminded her. "She was just as arrested as we were."

"*Summoned,* not *arrested,*" Beni sniffed. "We didn't break any laws! We aren't criminals." Her nose got red. The first tear leaked out. I wanted to shake her.

"Pull yourself together, Beni!" I hissed. "Everyone's

watching!" But I looked around and, luckily, no one was. Good thing, too, because within three seconds, Benita was in full-tilt, snot-running hysterics.

The temptation to smack her and yell "Snap out of it!" was nearly overwhelming. "We just have to come up with some witnesses for our side," I said as patiently as possible. "Who can you think of that'll say we never hardly picked on Poison Ivy?"

Beni wiped her soggy face.

"*Think!*" I said. "Does anyone owe you any favors?" But Beni was too busy falling apart to even listen.

Can you *believe* this?

IVY

Benita didn't sing the same song Sophie did about it being a case of mistaken identity. Her performance was equally creative, though, and I enjoyed it just as much. It happened between first and second period in front of the gym, when Benita sidled up to me, low and kind of sideways, like the bottom-feeding scavenger she is.

"Ivy," she said, "I want to apologize."

I put on my blank face and looked at her. She was shiny-nosed and red-eyed. She'd either been suffering from horrendous allergies or she'd been crying or she was in the early stages of some gooey eye disease that I could only hope was fatal.

I waited because it occurred to me that saying you *want* to apologize is not, strictly speaking, the same as actually apologizing. Eventually, Benita filled in the emptiness by saying, "I'm sorry."

Now, "I'm sorry" is nearly a full apology, and in most situations, it would do. But in this case, I needed to know what she was sorry for. Sorry she was born a parasitic sea crab? Sorry for all the misery she'd heaped on me over the years? Or sorry she got caught heaping?

Just a few days ago, I would've given anything to hear any one of The Evil Three apologize for anything. And for a second, I was tempted to forgive Benita, especially since her apology seemed pretty real. All Daria and I were suing for was for The Evil Three to leave me alone. But if Benita was willing to admit guilt and crawl on her belly to beg for my forgiveness, how could I resist?

I almost cracked a smile at the image of Benita dropping

to the floor at my feet, but I kept my face blank and tried my best to keep my voice neutral. Then I said, "This apology would've been more convincing *before* you got in trouble."

And Benita said, "I wanted to apologize lots and lots of times, but Annie wouldn't let me."

Oh. Wrong answer, I thought.

I knew Ann was the boss, but still, if Benita had fessed up and taken the blame that was hers to take, I probably would've dropped the case, whether Ms. Gold wanted to or not.

But the image of Benita bumping into me accidentally-on-purpose, then pretending to itch like crazy, scratching herself all over, yelling, "Oh no! I've got Poison Ivy!" was much clearer in my mind than this new show of regret.

It did occur to me, as I slid away from her, that The Evil Three might pool their money and have a contract put out on me. Hire a hit man and have me rubbed out. Or they could offer that same stash to me as a nice hefty bribe to forget the whole thing!

But better than cash was the pure satisfaction of watching both Benita and Sophie try to snivel out of this. Would Ann try next? Nah, she's not the groveling type. Ann was more likely to go down with guns blazing, fighting to the death. On the other hand, maybe I'm wrong. Maybe she, too, will come crawling. I'd give anything to see Ann beg.

BRYCE—Court reporter

Goldilocks hands me this cruddy old tape recorder and tells me I'm responsible for it and for the tapes until the end of the trial. Dude, the thing was a dinosaur, like ten times the size of yours. And see your little tapes? Hers were freaking monsters!

I go, "Whatever, dude."

At first, I don't see what the big stink is, till she says the jury'll probably need to listen to the tapes when they're deciding on the verdict. Then I get it—dude, she's warning me that those sly chicks might try and steal them! Or try and slip me false tapes or hit the erase button to mess with the evidence. Well, I'd just like to see them try!

They'll wear slinky clothes slit up to here and down to there, with those high-heeled shoes, and they'll lean all over me to try and wheedle into my secret stash of tapes.

But I'm cool. Cold even. No matter how hot things get, the tapes are safe. I'm in charge. Bond. James Bond.

First I've gotta figure out how to work this ancient warthog of a machine.

MARCO

My father was in a great mood after work, because his weight is down to 348. That probably doesn't sound like something to celebrate, but it is. You see, doctors' office scales stop at 350 pounds, so my dad, who'd always been big, hadn't been able to weigh himself till now. Three forty-eight took him off the zoo scale and put him among normal human fat people. He was excited and proud and in the mood to talk—so we talked about Ivy's harassment case.

"In America," my dad said, lining salad vegetables up on the counter, "we're *not* allowed to be on a jury if we know any of the people involved in the case. You have to recuse yourself."

"Recuse?"

"Yeah. Means to say, 'Sorry, but I'm not coming into this blank. He's my cousin's husband and I play squash with him every Saturday.' Or, 'The girl who got offed was my niece, so I wouldn't be terribly objective here.'" He raised the lettuce and scrutinized it.

"You'd have to excuse my whole class, pretty much," I said.

"Recuse," he corrected, handing me a tomato to wash and a few lettuce leaves to rewash. Then, over the sound of the water, he said, "In some other cultures, though, they see it differently. They believe you *have* to know a guy to be able to judge him fairly, and the skimpy details of an isolated incident are not enough to base a fair decision on. You have to take into account the guy's character, his temperament, his past, his family, and so forth."

I thought about that. My dad okayed my lettuce and handed me the cucumber.

"Your teacher should've staged a mediation instead of a trial," Dad said. "ADR—alternative dispute resolution—makes the two sides work together to settle their differences, whereas our current legal system forces people to keep as far apart as possible."

"I can't see Ann and her sidekicks working together with Ivy," I told him. "No way on earth."

Dad took the knife out of my hands and sliced the cucumber at an angle instead of straight down. These things still matter to him. Even if it's salad now instead of pasta.

"Then she could've used trial by ordeal," he said. "But first you gotta have a magic knife, one that knows all and sees the truth." He held up the cucumber knife and said, "Well! What do you know! This here's one!" He showed it to me and said, "You just heat this baby up over your campfire till it's good and hot. And you tell the poor sucker who's accused of the crime to open his mouth and stick out his tongue." My dad went back to slicing. "The theory is," he explained, "that if he's guilty, his mouth'll go dry and he'll be scared spitless. All you do is touch your hot knife to his tongue and *pfft!* It'll go up in smoke."

"They'd burn off the guy's tongue?" I asked. "Jeez!"

"Whereas, if the guy's *innocent* . . ." Dad pressed the cucumber knife to his own tongue, and grinned. "He'll have nothing to worry about and all that'll happen is maybe his saliva will sizzle a bit."

"What about the guy who's scared even though he's innocent?" I asked. "Like Einstein. She's not the one standing trial, but she's way more petrified up there than anyone else is. Her tongue would catch like kindling."

"Most systems are imperfect." Dad shrugged. Then he slammed a clove of garlic against the counter to smash it apart.

It was possible, I thought, that Benita and Sophie might feel guilty enough about their Ivy massacre to get singed to a lisp. But not Ann. I couldn't picture anything scaring her.

Talk about Ann, we were supposed to start the trial the next morning, but she took half the class time convincing Gold to let her dump Owen and be her own lawyer.

I figure that had something to do with how Ann and Owen used to be together. Did I already tell you about that? There wasn't a guy in school who wasn't as envious as all hell. I, for one, would have killed to be Owen. Until *pow!* Ann shut him out in the cold, and as far as I know, she never looked back.

Anyhow, Gold asked Ann if she'd ever heard the old saying that a lawyer who represents herself has a fool for a lawyer and a fool for a client.

"I've been called worse things than a *fool*," Ann answered, making everybody laugh. I knew she was standing tough, maybe hands on her hips, head thrown back, looking incredibly strong and sexy—so I didn't look at her. I was afraid the sight would have me sitting up and doing tricks again.

But you know what? I'd been keeping an eye out to see how Ann was working the other kids on the jury, and the truth is, I never saw her give any of them a single sniff. Wayne stood right behind her in line at the assembly, and I watched them the whole way into the auditorium—which I probably shouldn't admit if I don't want to sound like a stalker. I expected Ann to fling her hair at him at least, but she didn't.

Possibly, the image of Wayne Martin all lusted up just wasn't something Ann was willing to face. But the point is that Ann wasn't, in fact, constantly trying to seduce the *entire* jury.

Anyhow, once it was determined that Ann would be her own attorney and Benita and Sophie would stick with Owen, we got on with picking the jurors. But once Ann was in on the process, it turned into a different kind of circus. Now, getting picked for the jury became a popularity contest with Ann and Owen practically acting as game-show hosts.

Einstein should have been a factor in the vote, but she wasn't. I guess she figured that once she'd let Shannon slide, it hardly mattered what else she did.

Among those contestants vying for the few jury seats, no one lied as smoothly as Shannon had or was as blunt as Bryce. But even with everybody else falling somewhere in the middle, the process was a total joke.

Remember how, when you're little, people would tell you that winners never cheat and cheaters never win? Well, if my government class was a random sample of humanity, then forget it.

Anyhow, that poser Jennifer Puig got on the jury because Owen has the hots for her, and Ann likes the way she dresses. Owen chose his best friend, Kyle, next. Ann was fine with Kyle, too, which was a no-brainer because it was a safe bet that Kyle would do anything anyone more popular than him told him to.

But other than picking Kyle and Jennifer, Owen totally

got off on refusing people for the jury. It was a power thing. It came up and bit him in the ass, though, when he couldn't nix Wayne Martin.

I don't remember what Owen had asked him, but Wayne answered with one of his excruciatingly weird patriotic speeches. Something about the restoration of dignity being the something, something of every American citizen. I forget exactly. Over the top, as always, but still, I found Wayne's weirdo formality way easier to stomach than Owen's swaggering superiority.

"I refuse Wayne Martin," Owen sneered, turning his back on him.

Wayne jumped up and gasped, "That is an outrage!"

And Gold—who worships Wayne—said, "Sorry, Owen, you've already dismissed your allotted six. Remember?"

"What!" Owen squeaked, losing his faux-cool. Then he spun around, searching the class. "I'll trade!" he said. "Yes! I'll unrefuse Daniel Ornofrian and take *him* for the jury. That's it!" he sputtered. "I trade Daniel for Wayne!"

Gold smiled the happy little smile she wears when certain kids are miserable. "Sorry, Owen," she said. "There are no trades after the fact. A jury is not a deck of Pokemon cards. It's up to either Ann or Daria to determine Wayne's status at this point."

Einstein crept a few steps toward the front of the room to whisper that she had no objection to Wayne.

Then Ann bounded up and cheerfully announced, to Owen more than to anyone else, that she had no objection to Wayne Martin, either. "None at all," she said and batted her eyelashes in fake innocence at Owen. I don't think having Wayne Martin on the jury was in Ann's best interest, but I guess she figured it was worth it, just to piss Owen off—and it worked. Owen fumed as Wayne scuttled over to take the sixth juror chair.

It occurred to me that if this were the real world, and it was *me* on trial, I'd want weirdo Wayne on my jury. The guy is over the top, no question about it. You don't want to hang with him on weekends, and you don't want him on your team in any sport, but he isn't dumb and he isn't a flake.

He is the editor of the school paper and is always trying to stick real news and political issues in between the announcements of cake decorating fund-raisers for pom-poms and shots of Silly Hat Day. And he was the only soul who tried to get the debate club to duke it out over something meatier than the dress code. It is hopeless, of course, but you can't help admiring the guy for trying.

After Wayne came me. Or, as Gold spat it, "Unless Daria or Ann objects to Marco, he'll become juror number seven by default," meaning, *like it or not.*

Daria didn't object, of course. And Ann shot me one of those amazing smiles of hers. Then, looking me right in the eye, she said, "I'd be totally thrilled to have Marco!" I guess she thought having me on the jury would be another way to annoy Owen or whatever, like the Wayne Martin thing. But man, I gotta tell you, that girl can make *anything* sound sexy.

I thought being seventh made me the alternate, so I wouldn't have to do anything unless another kid on the jury dropped dead or quit school, but I was wrong. Gold said we wouldn't pick the alternate till later. She said that was so we'd *all* pay attention. What a low trick. I bet she made up that rule on the spot just to spite me.

DARIA

Never mind *Gentle's Holler*, the novel I'd been looking forward to curling up with all day. The main character is dirt poor and nearly starving to death with her blind baby sister and the rest of her huge mountain family, but I'd trade my problems for hers in a heartbeat. Tomorrow I had to present *opening statements*.

What was I supposed to say? What was I supposed to do with my hands? There was no desk or podium to stand behind. It would simply be me, out in the open with my arms waving around or hanging down, and everyone staring right at me.

According to Ms. Gold, our opening statements should introduce the jury to what they were going to hear and see during the course of the trial. But how did I know what they'd see? Ms. Gold said I should say something like, "The evidence will show that Ivy was cruelly victimized, et cetera."

I'd feel ridiculous standing up there, trying to talk phony legal-speak in front of everyone. The thought sucked the breath right out of my body.

I tried to trick myself by pretending it was just a written assignment, a paper. Unfortunately, I didn't fall for it. I simply could not write words, knowing I'd have to read them out loud. I confronted my blank screen for eons.

Then, just to do *something*, I ran a search on "Mock Trial, Sea View." I hopped absently from link to link until I suddenly found myself on Jennifer Puig's *My Space*, staring at my own name! This was it:

Owen with drama and passion
takes sides with the popular sluts,
Defending their right to be bitchy
without any ifs ands or butts.

While Einstein who's frigid and brittle,
as cold and as dry as a stick,
Locks arms with the loathed Poison Ivy
who makes all the rest of us sick.

I reeled, and cut the power.

Dry as a stick? *Frigid?*

Owen had passion but I was *frigid*? Does *quiet* have to equal *cold*? Was everyone supposed to be as horny and obvious as Owen and Ann were back when they were hooked up? Is that the passion Jennifer meant? Being an exhibitionist?

Ouch! Frigid? Brittle? Cold?

But who was spooky little Jennifer Puig to me? There was nothing original or passionate about her ripped black slips and inky dyed hair. Her entire look was imitation passion, white makeup, thick black eyeliner. And writing poetry, if you can call it that. How predictable.

But I'd never done a thing to her. Why had she felt the need to write about me like that? And wasn't it Jennifer, on the first day of court, who'd suggested I harvest Ann's vital organs? Hadn't we sort of laughed *together* over that?

I slumped over my keyboard, limp with shame.

How many other kids were reading Jennifer's poem? Were they adding slights of their own? I almost switched my computer back on to check, but I knew I wouldn't be able to take it.

By way of self-preservation, I forced myself up, away from my desk and out of my room, to stumble around the house. One of my brothers was practicing guitar in his room, the distortion amped high. It set my teeth on edge and perfectly echoed the clatter in my brain.

WAYNE MARTIN—Investigative Reporter

As the editor of *The Sea View Globe,* I was initially compelled to raise my pen and respond journalistically to this outrage masquerading as education in Ms. Gold's third-hour American Government class.

As a juror, however, I was silenced by the restriction on discussing the case. That restriction holds true for the written, as well as the spoken, word.

I realize that being a juror is a key position from which to mete out true justice to the foes of freedom. Nonetheless, I feel like a man who has lost his voice.

Therefore, I have taken up this online journal and plan to document the case as it unfolds.

DARIA

I hope Ms. Gold gets fired over this. I know that's unkind, but she really should. Look at all the unhappiness she brewed up in her witch's cauldron. Mine, for sure, but Ivy's too, and . . . Well, even if no one else was suffering through this trial, *my* misery counts for something.

Ms. Gold might as well have written Jennifer's poem herself. I never would've come to Jennifer's attention if Ms. Gold hadn't forced me on her.

I don't understand people like her. I really don't. Her job is to teach American Government, not to muck around in her students' lives. But if she was attentive enough to notice my dread of public speaking, why didn't she honor it? If anything, my shyness should get me excused from things like this. Other handicaps are treated with consideration and respect.

People like Ms. Gold think shyness is a choice. But honestly, who would *choose* to be phobic? Who would *choose* to be stricken with debilitating fear and neurosis? You'd have to be crazy!

And perhaps I am.

I'm willing to accept that it's a mental illness. I'd be perfectly content to be labeled as nuts, crazy, insane, cuckoo, psycho, cracked, bonkers, boffo, wacko, loony, batty, gorked, demented—*anything*—if it would get me excused from all future public speaking. I'm entirely serious.

Especially something like this, which has no script, no notes to hold on to or read from. No marked beginning, middle, or end. Just me, out there, making it up as I go along, endlessly alone, naked in front of strangers.

My mom, on the other hand, thought the whole thing sounded great. She was delighted that the mean girls were being forced to face up to their sins for once. And she loved it that the picked-on kid would finally get to have her say.

I knew my mom was imagining the class trial as one marvelous growth opportunity. Not the sickening, tumorous, malignant growth that it is in reality, but the spring-green, blossoming-as-a-person kind. The kind where we'd all see ourselves and others with new clarity and compassion and become better people.

I could practically turn the pages in my mind. The bad girls, Ann and her crowd, would be sorry, sorry, sorry by the end of the story. Perhaps they'd become nurses or nuns and spend the rest of their lives performing selfless acts of charitable kindness.

Ivy, of course, would suddenly be revealed as a beauty and wit, beloved and admired by all.

And the Daria character? Well, although I'd start out as my gangly, tongue-tied self, I'd no doubt evolve into a brilliant spokesperson for the underdog. Saving the day with my inspired speeches and legal insights. Thus marking the onset of what would unfold as my remarkably successful legal career.

My mom was looking at me as if it was foregone that I'd triumph in this role, hailed as the hero, carried out of the classroom/courtroom on the shoulders of my cheering classmates.

But I'm not even remotely interested in being a lawyer.

I don't know what I *do* want to be, but I'm positive it doesn't involve courts or law or bossing people around or arguing. And most importantly, it does not entail getting up in front of people. Of that I am *beyond* sure.

My poor mom. She loves me. She does. I believe that. But she doesn't get me at all.

I wasn't ready to return to my stuffy room or the sight of the computer screen where Jennifer Puig's insults had burned their image. I didn't want to tell my mom about the poem, but I couldn't just make small talk about my younger brother's acne or my older brother's girlfriend, either. So I said, "If *you* were accused of being so mean that you had to stand trial in front of the entire class, wouldn't you be humiliated?"

Mom nodded.

"Well, not Ann," I said. "She just gets up and flounces around without a thought. I don't know how she can face the class."

My mom shook her head. "Daria, I assure you that Ann is dying on the inside. Trust me. She's just putting on a brave front."

I looked at her with disbelief.

"Seriously," Mom said. "You don't know how she feels alone at night. The poor kid probably hates herself."

I knew my mother was wrong, but what good was trying to convince her?

When I told her that Ivy didn't like the word *plaintiff* because it sounded too complainy—like *complaintiff*—Mom thought that was clever and suggested I take a closer look at Ivy. "She may be the soulmate you've been waiting for," Mom said, "in disguise."

"Disguised as an annoying space cadet with a sinus infection," I grumbled.

"Now Daria, there's no call for cattiness!" Mom snapped, and I knew our chat was over.

First my bedroom, now the den. I was running out of rooms, and my brother's music was starting to feel like a personal assault. I stepped out the back door and the cold concrete of the steps brought an instant feeling of clarity straight up from my bare feet to my brain. There were no stars, of course, but the outdoors felt so big it helped me shrink to an unimportance that I could handle. It always helps me to feel small and invisible. I feel it when I'm lost in a novel—and I feel it outside, at night. Why do I always forget that?

What I'd taken as night-silence got quieter still when the neighbor's sprinkler shut off with a moan. Under that layer of sound were the crickets. Under the crickets, was the distant freeway. And under that? Peace.

The Jennifer Puigs and the Ms. Golds shrank down to specks out in the darkness and were carried off on the night air. I felt small and safe, cleansed by the evening chill, and soothed by the fragrance of night-blooming jasmine.

My mind cleared.

Obviously, it wasn't about winning or losing the case. So there had to be more to it. But what? Essentially, everyone in school had seen those girls tease Ivy countless times. They hadn't been sneaky about their meanness. It was right out there, center stage. That meant that as soon as I called on anyone in the class and put them under oath, that would be the end of the trial.

Like, if I asked Marco . . . no, not Marco because he was on the jury, but say, Cameron. Well, not Cameron because he's new and doesn't seem to pay much attention. But if I asked *anyone* else if they'd seen Ann bullying Ivy, they'd have to say yes.

Was my job to get a whole chorus line of kids to stand in front of the jury and chant in unison that they'd witnessed Ann and her friends' cruelty? I guess on a really basic level, I simply didn't get it. It seemed too easy.

Not that I wanted to round up witnesses and herd them to the front of the room or be the one to choreograph the whole war-crimes tribunal, but still, everyone had seen Ann pick on Ivy. And I mean *everyone.*

I thought I should count my blessings: one. At least I wasn't Ann, Benita, and Sophie's attorney. I couldn't imagine how Owen would be able to find a single soul who hadn't seen Ann be mean. Unless, of course, other kids were willing to lie the way Shannon had. But that didn't seem likely. Shannon was a special case. She'd always been on the fringes of Ann's crowd, trying to claw and elbow her way in.

I remember back in third or fourth grade, Shannon used to steal things for Ann as gifts. Bribes. Ann would go to the Mini Mart to make her selection, and then put in her order with Shannon. We all knew it.

I took a few slow breaths of cool night air and closed my eyes, deepening the darkness. My arms were all goose bumps and my shoulders were hunching with cold. I no longer dreaded my hot, stuffy bedroom.

I unclenched my jaw and enjoyed a final shiver before going back inside.

I resolved to get to school early the next morning and make myself gather up a few kids to be witnesses. The prospect of standing in front of everyone was grim. Especially if they'd all read Jennifer Puig's "poem." But at least it should be fairly straightforward and quick. I'd get through my opening statements. Then call on my witnesses, who would say what they saw. The jury would vote and that would be it. In, out, done.

FRIDAY

Opening Statements

BRYCE

First, Einstein calls Ivy her *client,* like she's getting paid. Then I don't hear nothing else that chick says. She's so damn quiet. Just stands there, as breakable as a Frito, lips barely moving, not hardly any sound coming out, reading off her little card. Then she goes reeling back to her seat like she's been hit by a stun gun. Dude, it's pitiful.

Owen gets up next, struts around, and cracks his pie-hole to say everyone knows these girls are rotten, no-good slime. That cracks everyone up, except for Ann and Benita and Sophie, who start hollering and screaming and one thing and another.

Till, *bam!* The door slams against the wall. And there's Broccoli with her demon scowl. You know her, the principal?

And she goes, "Dude! What's all the racket?"

Goldilocks scurries over to explain and Broccoli marches her into the hall to get reamed.

Turns out, Broccoli puts the squelch on the trial, says we gotta get parental autographs before we can go on. Goldilocks is gonna print permission slips and we gotta stop by later to get one. That's our entire homework for Monday. *Sweet!*

Goldilocks writes her *home* phone number on the board and says any parents with questions are welcome to call. Then she makes us lug out our books and reread some dog-meat chapter on the court system or some rot, so I resume my tally. See those holes in the ceiling? I'm counting them. There's eighteen across by twelve down on each panel. The secret is you gotta subtract for lights and smoke detectors. Not everyone thinks of that!

IVY

I wasn't nearly the wreck Daria was. She was a sea anemone, quivering in the current, ready to retract at the least touch. It hurt to watch her, but with Daria you couldn't hear her if you didn't look at her. Half the trick was reading her lips.

For such a famous brain, I hadn't noticed her coming up with anything all that brilliant for my case. Maybe *I* should've been *her* lawyer and we could've sued over her being called Einstein, which is as bad as being called Poison Ivy, almost.

I knew I should be listening harder, but I got distracted by a ladybug on the edge of the aquarium. She'd walk awhile on her hair-thin legs, then stop to think her ladybug thoughts. Sometimes she'd wave a leg or two over the edge, then straighten her course and creep on. The suspense was intense. If she fell in, would Ms. Gold's goldfish eat her? Did she realize that the end of her world was possibly no more than one tiny bug step off the ledge? I barely blinked—afraid if I glanced away for even a split second, she'd disappear and I'd never know if she'd flown away or been eaten or what.

Meanwhile, Daria's opening statements were so stiff and weird, she practically sounded like Wayne Martin. Well, a very, very *quiet* Wayne Martin.

"My client"—I'd asked Daria not to call me the *plaintiff,* because it sounds so pathetic—"has been the victim of intentional emotional cruelty for years at the hands of the codefendants, Ann, Sophie, and Benita. In retribution, we ask that the jury find the codefendants liable and award my client a guarantee of no further abuse. We seek a restraining order that would keep the codefendants from coming within ten feet of my client. And we ask for a written apology. Thank you."

Then Daria scuttled back to the seat next to me and retracted her quivering anemone tentacles into a tight knot of terror.

Next, Owen lobster walked to the front of the room and said his defendants, Sophie and Benita, were mere sheep compared to Ann. Mindless followers.

I thought he was going to say that they were innocent because they weren't as guilty as Ann, but he didn't. Instead, he said that sure, Sophie and Benita were mean, but they were just *medium* mean, nothing extraordinary. He said they weren't any meaner to me than everyone is to someone, which is *not* true. I'm not mean to anyone and I never have been, except when I was so little that I didn't know better.

Then Owen said I deserved it anyway for dressing weird.

Until then I'd have sworn Owen had never noticed me or the way I dressed—not that I was flattered by his attention. But lawyers are often called sharks, and Owen was obviously happy to rip the flesh from my bones and cloud the water with my billowing blood. His final attack was that it was really my parents' fault for naming me Ivy. Owen suggested it was them I should sue.

The next thing I knew, the principal, Miss Brock, with her giant down-turned tuna mouth, whooshed in and dragged my little teacher into the hall.

Poor Ms. Gold, wiggling like fresh bait. I wondered if she'd lose her job because of me and have to live on the streets wearing plastic garbage bags and begging money in front of the Von's market on Sunset. Those women amaze me. I heard somewhere that they aren't as old as they look. It's just that living on the streets is so hard it makes them age fast. Maybe I won't even recognize Ms. Gold once her hair goes stringy and she gets that look in her eyes that they all seem to have.

But for now, the Brock/Gold distraction made me glance away from my ladybug, and sure enough, when I looked back, she was gone.

Figures.

MARCO

Owen started his defense by saying Sophie and Benita were no meaner than anyone else. "We're all mean to someone," he said. "A little brother, a kid on the bus, some twerp at camp."

For a second, I thought he almost had a point, but then he said, "Add to that the fact that Ivy's got a way of getting on people's nerves, and even if it really bites, it's not anyone's fault. It's not about blame. It's just reality."

Owen is an idiot, but still, the idea that there was nowhere to hide in this life if you were Ivy gave me chills. As if the fates had it in for her and the rest of us were only fulfilling our predetermined destinies as her tormentors.

There was some muttering around the room, but that's all it was, *muttering*. No one, myself included, did anything to challenge Owen. Even Gold just sat there. I told you that woman was cold.

Maybe it was a freedom-of-speech thing, but gimme a break. The whole point of this trial was that the Anns were not supposedly free to say mean things to Ivy. So why was Owen? Plus, it seems to me that if Owen was allowed to say mean things, then Ivy should be allowed not to listen to them. But she wasn't free to ditch class—not that she looked like she wanted to. In fact, if anything, Ivy looked bored! How weird is *that*?

If she'd flinched, or shown some sign of life, maybe Gold would've pulled Owen off her. But Ivy just gazed into the fish tank and gave no hint of human reaction. Same as when Ann teased her. I guess it's a "don't let 'em see you sweat" thing.

That was my dad's advice to me when I was little, back

when he used to lecture me on how to deal with bullies. I guess he assumed I'd be picked on. His entire childhood sounded like one long battle, probably because of being fat. It must blow his mind that I've never been in a fight.

If someone did want to fight me, though, I wouldn't take my dad's advice. When Ivy does the no-reaction thing, it just seems to make the Anns push even harder for a reaction. Isn't that what they're after? Proof of their strength and your weakness? Isn't that what makes it fun for them?

I like to think that if someone wanted to fight me, I'd just kill him. But who knows.

Anyhow, Owen held up his hand, cop-style, and the muttering stopped. He was so stoked that he wasn't even surprised to be obeyed. His next bit was that Ivy's parents were to blame for naming her Ivy in the first place.

"They must have known there's not a kid alive who could resist at least thinking of her as *Poison* Ivy," Owen said.

Just that morning at breakfast, my dad had thumped the newspaper and said that his fellow fat men were looking for someone to sue for their girth. He read, "Fast food restaurants are to blame for their portion size, and their use of low-cost, high-fat ingredients."

Dad snorted and slid the page over to me. "Everything is always someone else's fault," he spat.

I skimmed the article while my dad continued to rant about what a spineless species we are. Finally, he pushed his oatmeal aside and grandly announced to my mom and me that he is obese because he eats like a pig and does no exercise. "It's no one's fault but my own!" he confessed.

My mom barely looked up to pat his hand and say, "We know that, dear." And we all laughed.

Now, here was Owen blaming everybody except the girls who did the actual bullying. First it was Ivy's parents' fault that everybody picked on their daughter. Next he blamed Ivy herself, saying if she cared so much about what the other girls thought of her, she would take the trouble to dress better. Then, he jammed his fists in his pockets and said, "I rest my case."

That made Jeremy haul off and clobber his desk. "You can't rest your case before you've even started!"

Owen answered, "I started, and I finished. I'm done."

Sophie jumped up on her hind legs. "Hey!" she wailed. "What about telling them how *I* wasn't really part of it?"

Then Ann got up and shoved Owen aside. She faced us on the jury and said, "*Poison Ivy* is the name of a totally hot character in the Batman movies. And I, for one, would be flattered out of my mind if anyone called *me* by her name!"

Then in marched principal Brock, foaming at the mouth in a bureaucratic lather over needing permission slips signed in triplicate by our guardians.

It was weird, the whole thing. I don't know about anyone else, but I felt a little shaky the rest of the day—like I'd witnessed a hit-and-run.

DARIA

It was so excruciating for Ivy to be discussed and dissected like that that she spent the entire time picking nonexistent lint off her shirt and pretending to watch the fish. I don't think she even glanced in the direction of the trial. I sympathize. If she felt even a fraction of the misery I did up there, then her life was agony. It was like standing in front of a firing squad—except that this execution was in s-l-o-w motion.

I made myself peek at Cameron, the process server, to see if he was nauseated by the sight of me—but he was sound asleep! I thought that was so funny. If I hadn't been sick with panic, I would've laughed.

Imagine being relaxed enough to sleep in public. Perhaps it was because he ran track and was tired. I wish I could be that calm and laid back. He is even popular already and he only moved here at the end of last year. That's partly because he is cute, of course, but also because he is so easygoing.

I bet he thought I was ugly. I bet he thought I was a pathetic loser.

I glued my eyes back down to the notecard where I'd written my opening statement. The words went in through my eyes and out through my lips without passing my brain at all. I know I probably sounded like a robot, but at least I made it through without having a heart attack.

Next, Owen presented some survival-of-the-fittest Darwinian argument that was really sick. Basically, he said that it was perfectly natural for superior, carnivorous beasts like Ann's crowd to feed on inferior creatures like poor Ivy.

It was vaguely Nazi-like, now that I think of it. Almost like a defense of a master race.

Then Owen stepped aside, and Ann pranced up to the front, like a circus pony, tossing her mane. I was still too stunned by Owen's cruelty to really focus on Ann, but I believe she began by saying something about Batman.

Then a miracle happened! Until that moment, I'd never been a huge fan of our principal, Ms. Brock, because she has a "shoot now, ask questions later" toughness about her. But she became my hero.

Every cell in my being prayed that no one would get their releases signed and we could abandon the entire court fiasco forever, and I'd never have to get up in front of that class again. Amen.

THE WEEKEND
Court Recess

ANN—Codefendant

First, I should tell you that we made up—us and Soph. IMing half the night, Beni and Sophie mostly. That was a scene in itself, but I don't feel like going into it right now, because *Marco* is driving me *crazy*! I can't figure that boy out!

Have you talked to him yet? Did he say anything about *me*?

Okay, never mind.

But from the way he ignored me in science, you'd swear he'd never walked me to class or told me all that stuff about Clingers. Still, I was pretty sure he'd call that night. In fact, I'd been half expecting him to be waiting for me after class or after school at least, but *nothing. Not a thing!* No e-mail; not even a note in my locker.

Then the next day, too, a big, bloody *nothing*! I must've blown it. But how? I'd been so nice to him!

Meanwhile, that stupid court thing was so *annoying*! Everyone was having a grand old time totally at *my* expense. It's *amazing* what I put up with. Seriously.

Later, Soph called and said, "My da"—she saw some Irish or Scottish movie where they called their dads *Da*, so now she does, too, although it sounds entirely phony. But anyway, she goes, "My da won't sign, so that's that."

"That's *what*?"

"Well, that stupid trial can't go on and we can go back to normal."

"*Wrong*," I said. "Remember? If we don't do the trial, we do Broccoli, and she'll suspend us in a blink."

"My da's going to school."

"For what?" I asked.

"To talk to Broccoli."

"To get you off the hook? Is he gonna tell her you just happened to get trapped in a ten-car pileup?" I asked. "And I suppose your *da*'s gonna tell her *I* was driving the big rig that started it all."

I could tell I nailed it there, because from her end of the line came nothing but sweaty air and bad breath. Then she half changed the subject and asked me what *my* mother said. Right. As if I showed her the permission slip. That would be just as bad as getting suspended. My mother would pitch a fit.

"Mine was signed before we even left school," I explained.

"You forged your mom's name?" she asked.

"No," I explained. "I didn't forge my *mom*'s name. I signed my *da*'s."

Oooh, that really got her because she knows no one's heard from my dad in months. Stumped and stupefied, Soph went back to breathing.

Why do I even *bother*? That's what *I'd* like to know.

IVY

Mom made me repeat about fifty times that I was suing three popular girls in class. She couldn't get her mind around one thing in particular: *How did I expect to get accepted into the popular crowd if I acted like that?*

When I tried to explain that I had as much chance of being part of that group as a frog has of flying, Mom put her hands over her ears.

Then when I said, for the hundredth time, that I have no interest in being friends with them, because they're *mean,* I may as well have been speaking Armenian.

On the bus home, I'd been thinking that this trial was yet another mistake. I never should've let Ms. Gold talk me into it. When she found my note, I should've laughed or said it wasn't mine. Snatched it away from her and crumpled it up. Or shredded it into tiny pieces and swallowed them. At least I wish I hadn't spilled the story of The Evil Three, because now it was flooding its banks and turning murky. I half decided it was time to pull the plug on the whole thing by *not* getting my permission slip signed. Let it circle the drain and be gone.

But if I won, then Ann and her coven wouldn't be allowed anywhere near me: that heaven would be well worth this bit of ugliness. And if they really were kept from ever speaking to me again, that would be peace everlasting. Also, I was dying—pardon the pun—to see their letter of apology.

"But Ivy," Mom insisted, "they aren't going to like you if you're resentful and sour-faced all the time! You have to smile! Laugh! Be fun!" She breezed her arms around in demonstration.

"I don't want them to like me," I said as patiently as I could. "I want them to leave me alone."

"Don't be silly," she scoffed. "If you just act friendly, they are sure to notice and—"

I interrupted her. "Trust me, Ma, it's not going to happen."

I wanted to tell her to shut up, but that would make her cry and then I'd have to spend the next ten hours apologizing and trying to comfort her, and promising to laugh merrily with Ann and Benita and Sophie when they say vicious things to and about me.

I didn't tell my mother to shut up; I did something worse: I told her what Owen said about it being my parents' fault for giving me such a poisonous name.

It was as if I'd slugged her with my fist. Really, the force of my words practically knocked her over, and it did actually spill her tea on the tablecloth. She sopped it up, sponging in desperate little stabs, and gasped, "Your *name*? You're not popular because of your *name*?"

She was so overcome with whatever it was she was overcome by—guilt? hopelessness? exhaustion?—that eventually she gave up and signed the stupid permission slip.

MONDAY

Examination and Cross-Examination

DARIA

When I got to school, I saw Wayne Martin standing in front of my locker. The closer I got to him, the more I felt my vertebrae compress, crunching me shorter.

"Good morning, Daria," he snapped in his ever-efficient, man-on-important-business tone. Then he handed me a sheet of blue paper and said, "I'd appreciate it if you'd take a look at an essay I've written."

An essay? I was confused. Why should Wayne want me to read his essay? I thought it might be for the newspaper or something. In any event, here it is. Sorry, it's a little wrinkled.

Is Today's Youth Basically Good?
or
Is Our Intrinsic Nature Evil?

I am sure I speak for most of us when I say that I am insulted and repulsed by Owen Anderson's depiction of the youth of today. His statements in Ms. Gold's third hour are founded on the blatant misconception that all minds are as distorted as his. His "defense" of Ann, Benita, and Sophie evokes a worldview so pessimistic and cynical that it is nearly sociopathic!

Owen's assumption that everyone our age is mean-spirited and given to random acts of cruelty is simply WRONG. I, for one, believe today's youth is BETTER than that. I believe we have learned from the mistakes of past generations and that we strive for goodness and human decency!

The true case is that although a FEW of us may have strayed (for reasons known only to themselves) down a path of dissregard for their fellow Americans' feelings, most of us staunchly uphold an honorable belief in kindness and compassion and fair treatment for all!

I read it twice with Wayne practically standing at attention beside me. After the first read-through, I understood that he thought he was *helping* me in some way with the trial.

I looked at him standing so stiffly, with his lips pursed in his superior, know-it-all way.

"You misspelled *disregard*," I said, pretending that I thought he was showing it to me for editing. "Otherwise, it's not bad."

I think he was shocked, and actually, I was fairly surprised myself. But it felt good—and bad—to be a little mean to him. I tried to hand him back his essay but he wouldn't take it, so I slipped it into my folder. Then I turned to open my locker, hoping he'd get the hint that he should leave, which he did.

But his essay had made its point: I was failing miserably as Ivy's lawyer.

BRYCE

The first thing Goldilocks says is, "I want to thank anyone who didn't call me over the weekend. . . . If there is, in fact, anyone who didn't call."

Ha-ha. I guess her phone rang a lot. Not *all* of 'em were me.

A load of kids forgot their releases, but Sophie was the only one actually *in* the trial, and it's not that she forgot hers, it's that her folks said "No friggin' way, dude!" and refused to sign.

But instead of killing the whole show, Goldilocks leaves the non-release kids in the audience, and signals me to crank up my machine. Righty-o! I point its runty microphone in the direction of the action and go, "Dude! Let the wild rumpus begin!"

Ann gets up and reminds us that she's representing her own hot little self. Hey, there's not a guy in the room wouldn't give all he's got to *represent* her, if you know what I mean. Even if she is a pain.

It's criminal, dude, how chicks never look on the outside the way they are on the inside. It sure would make life a lot easier for the rest of us if they did.

MARCO

Gold wasn't going to let a little thing like parental refusal stop her from staging her beloved trial—even though Sophie was one of the kids whose parents didn't sign.

Gold just dragged a chair up to the witness box and said, "From now on, this chair represents Sophie." Then she told us to hustle to our court places.

"We left off with Ann's opening statements," she said. "Ann has chosen to dismiss Owen, as you recall, and she will be representing herself."

Ann stood in front of the class, wearing the shortest skirt I'd ever seen in real life. She said, "Your honor"—which Jeremy loved—"Ladies and gentlemen of the jury, I think the plaintiff, Ivy Smith, is making *way* too big a stink out of this thing. And I've got just one thing to say to her and Einstein, I mean *Daria,* and that is, *prove it!*" Then Ann tossed her mane and turned back to her seat, all attitude and legs.

Einstein was up next, and I'm telling you, it's painful to watch that girl. She's not just shy, she's pathologically shy. Gold didn't show her a speck of mercy, though. She just let Daria cringe like a beaten dog. Not that I've ever seen a beaten dog, but you know what I mean.

No, wait. I take that back. I *have* seen beaten-looking dogs, lots of them, in Mexico. Skinny yellow dogs, dusty and sort of low in the tail, with saggy tits hanging down like they'd had a million puppies.

I remember one time, we were sitting on a stone wall in Oaxaca, eating quesadillas from a little stand. My father was very seriously into quesadillas on that trip. Anyhow, this scabby dog, scrawny as death, came cringing over to beg, and it looked so miserable it made me sick.

Don't get me wrong, I love dogs. And most times, if a dog gives me those eyes, I'm a total sucker. But this was different.

I guess my dad could tell what I was thinking, or maybe I said something, I don't know. But he said, "That's the problem with hunger and homelessness and poverty in general. It's not pretty. And it's hard to care about repulsive-looking sufferers."

He hadn't meant to make me feel bad, but it stung anyhow, so I gave that dog the rest of my food. I didn't feed it to her, though. I tossed it on the ground way over there.

My mom threw it her scraps, too, and within seconds, a whole bunch of messed-up-looking dogs appeared. We were surrounded by them.

Nonetheless, my dad held on to every bit of his quesadilla, and sat there licking his fingers when he was done. That doesn't necessarily mean anything about his philosophy of life. He's a big guy and takes his food hyperseriously. But the point is that none of those dogs begged in the usual way. They didn't wag their tails or look hopeful or optimistic. They just stood there being skinny and grim. It was eerie.

Sorry. That was random. But Einstein was a lot like those dogs. You feel awful for her, but you don't want to scratch behind her ears or let her lick your face or whatever.

DARIA

Four kids failed to bring their releases! Sophie among them.
I almost cheered out loud. Prayers answered!

Then Ms. Gold began arranging the furniture into the
courtroom configuration and said we were going to go ahead
regardless.

What? What was with this woman? Why was she so
determined to have this trial?

I felt ill.

Ann got up and addressed the class, but unfortunately,
the school didn't burst into flames before she sat back down.

Ms. Gold told me to call my first witness, but I didn't
have one. You don't know me well enough to get how
unusual it was for me to come to class unprepared. I'm not
the type to blow off homework. And I'm no rebel. So it's
hard, if not impossible, for me to understand, let alone
explain, how I came to be in this situation.

I simply hadn't arranged with anyone to speak. It was
not a conscious omission, nor had it slipped my mind. I'd
just somehow convinced myself that Principal Brock's
request for releases would be the death of the whole misbe-
gotten project.

So there I was, with absolutely nothing planned and a
pounding in my head that made me feel like blood was
going to gush out of my eyes. And now I had to scan frantically around the room for someone to call on.

Kids looked at me sideways, peeking up from under
their hair. Some held books in front of their faces to avoid
my gaze. Of course, no one wanted to be called on. I
wouldn't have either.

Time went into one of those elongating, twisting things like it does in nightmares.

Finally, Ms. Gold said, "Perhaps you'd like to call Ivy?"

And I gratefully said, "Yes! Ivy, will you take the stand, please?"

And she did.

Ms. Gold made Ivy raise her right hand and put her left hand on our American Government textbook. Then she had to swear to tell the truth.

Jeremy made her state her name.

Then it was back to me. In one giddy flash that almost reduced me to cackling insanity, it occurred to me that at least now that I was exposed as being stupid, everyone might finally stop calling me Einstein.

But my hysterics were halted before they began by one peek at Wayne Martin in the jury box. He sat straight-backed and fierce. His beady little eyes piercing me like needles. I recalled his essay and could even see the blue of the paper in my mind, but I couldn't fathom how all that philosophizing about the nature of humankind could help me now.

Eventually, I muddled through, although it could hardly have gone worse. I asked Ivy to point to the people who were mean to her, because I'd seen that done on television. She pointed to Ann, then Benita, and then the chair that was supposed to be Sophie. That made half the class laugh.

Ivy certainly didn't make it any easier. Here was her chance to have her say, her opportunity to get out whatever she'd had in mind when she agreed to be Gold's pet lawsuit. But when I asked her if there was anything she wanted to mention, Ivy simply shrugged, making us both look like dummies and giving the class something else to laugh about.

Next, I asked Ivy something like, "Wouldn't you like to tell us how they were mean?"

And she shook her head and said, "Not really."

Not really? My brain shrieked. What do you mean *not really*? What am I doing up here then? But I didn't scream or slap her. I simply asked her, practically begged her, to please describe how she'd been mistreated.

"They'd follow me down the hall," she said, her tone flat, her face expressionless. Then she added, "They said mean things."

I wanted to strangle her. "Can you be more specific?" I asked.

Ivy shrugged and said, "You know what they did. You all saw them," which was true, but somehow it made her sound like a lunatic.

I limped on from there, but the class, meanwhile, slipped quickly out of control. Everyone was talking, laughing. Once or twice, Ms. Gold asked the class to be more respectful, but she didn't demand it. I kept expecting her to come to her senses and put an end to the whole atrocity, but she never did. It didn't seem possible that this was what she'd had in mind from the start, unless she was seriously twisted.

Periodically Jeremy banged on his desk, shouting, "Order in the court!" Perhaps that was his way of trying to help me, but it only managed to make everything even wilder and more chaotic.

Eventually I slunk away and left Ivy to Owen's cross-examination, which was awful, of course. As if the things he'd said last week in his opening statements weren't hurtful enough, this time he began by asking her if she'd ever been called Poison Ivy in her last school.

Ivy answered, "Yes. By Ann, Sophie, and Benita." Then she did that gross sinus thing she does, and it made me wince. I don't know if anyone else noticed, though, because I couldn't make myself look up.

"I meant before that," Owen said. "Wherever you went to school before you moved here."

"I moved here in fourth grade," Ivy said. "When I was nine."

Owen was getting annoyed, and I could feel that the class was on his side. He asked her, with exaggerated patience, whether anyone had called her Poison Ivy at her old school in third grade or second or first or kindergarten or preschool.

And plucking frantically at her sweater, she mumbled, "Yes."

"In which one?" Owen asked, grinning. "Fourth?"

"Yes."

"Third?"

Even quieter, "Yes."

"Second?"

And out of nowhere, I said, "I object!" Everyone was surprised, but no one was as surprised as me.

Jeremy pounded his desk and said, "Einstein objects!"

"Her name is Daria," Ms. Gold corrected him. "And you're supposed to ask her on what grounds—*why* she objects," Ms. Gold told him.

So Jeremy roared, "On what grounds?"

"Torturing my client?" I asked.

"Correct!" Ms. Gold cheered. "Badgering a witness." She told Owen to get to the point.

"My point, *Ivy*," Owen said, "is that you should be used to it by now. Did you sue them in your old school?"

Right then, Bryce let out a groan.

"No moaning in the court!" Jeremy said. You could tell he'd meant it to sound deep and thunderous, but his voice cracked.

It turned out that Bryce had forgotten to put a cassette in the tape recorder.

"Lock him up!" Jeremy tried again, banging his desk with his fist. "Abuse of government property!"

Ms. Gold and Bryce fiddled around with the machine, but by the time they'd rewound the tape, the bell had rung and class was over. That was good, and bad. I dreaded going on with this, but at least I'd make sure to have some questions prepared for tomorrow and witnesses to call.

FAITH

I hate Daria! Everyone thinks she's so ladylike and gentle but trust me, it's all an act. You should've seen how she cornered me and bullied me and—you laugh, but I swear it's true! Here's what happened: I was walking down the hall, minding my own business—actually, I was racing down the hall because I had to pee—when Daria grabbed me. Well, maybe not *grabbed,* but you know, she touched me at least and I stopped because I was surprised. We hadn't talked in ages. Not that we had a fight or anything; we'd never been good enough friends to fight. But for whatever reason, I was surprised, until she got around to asking me if I'd take the witness stand. She said, "All you'd have to do is explain how Ann, Benita, and Sophie treat Ivy."

My first reaction was to say no. But Daria wouldn't let it go at that. And I'll tell you something, she has always been rather pushy in her own mousy way. I swear, I remember that about her. When we worked together on a project for history, it was pretty much everything her way. She was quiet about it, but there was no question that her way was the right and only way, according to her. But we got an A+ (my first and only) on the stupid thing, so why spit?

As I was saying, Daria wouldn't take no for an answer. She stayed on me, reminding me of the time last year when Ann wrote that mean stuff on the board about Ivy. Daria practically backed me against the wall, going on about our sixth-grade retreat and the stuff Ann and Benita and Sophie did to Poison Ivy's bed, and all that. I couldn't look her in the eye. Daria, I mean. Because she practically made it sound like the whole thing was my fault, which is crazy.

That's what I mean by being a bully. Don't let her little voice and all her shy little ways fool you!

I didn't want to have anything to do with this trial and that doesn't make me *bad*. It's not like Daria volunteered either, you know. I'm positive that if Ms. Gold had asked Daria if she wanted to be Ivy's attorney, Daria would've said "No way!" (politely and quietly, of course). But misery loves company or whatever, so Daria was trying to guilt me into this mess with her.

Maybe it would've been different if this were a real court, but it's not like this trial was serious, with Jeremy as the judge making so much noise and Bryce forgetting to turn on his tape recorder and Sophie being a chair. In fact, Daria might be the only one who's taking this stupid thing to heart. Even Ivy herself looks like her mind is a million miles away half the time.

But how do I tell someone as low on the food chain as Daria that I can't afford to sacrifice myself? That my standing in school is low enough already, thank you very much, and any lower would be underground—like her. Maybe Daria doesn't care that she's a total geek, but I do! How do I tell a person like Daria that whatever good this trial might (and I mean *might*) do for Ivy, it'll do way more harm to me. It would be social suicide to take Ivy and Daria's side against everyone who matters.

And it's not *my* fault Daria got trapped.

It's like the statues of the three mammoths at the La Brea Tar Pits. Have you seen them? One huge guy is caught in the tar. His head is thrown back with his tusks in the air, and you can tell he's yelling for help. But nothing moves. He's stuck forever, sinking, and his wife and kid are stuck forever watching from shore. It's incredibly sad and creepy, especially since you know that all of them went totally extinct. Including the baby.

But Daria kept pushing me—I don't mean physically pushing, but practically begging me to wade into the bottomless black tar with her. I really had to pee, so just to get away, I said I'd think about it. Daria smiled as if I'd said I'd do it. But I didn't say any such thing, I swear! I said I'd *think*! And what I thought was, For now I'm safe on the shore, and I'm staying out of that tar as long as I can!

CAMERON—Process Server

I was bare-buns in the locker room when someone said there was a girl out there says she's gotta talk to me. Everyone made their jungle noises, so I pulled on my shorts and ducked my head out. It was that envelope girl from class, looking at her shoes again.

I go, "You lookin' for me?"

And she said, "Yeah," but real quietlike. "I need you to serve more papers, if that's okay."

I remembered how ticked Annie got about the last one. But I go, "Sure," because this poor girl looked so scared. The kind of scared like a bird that fell outta the nest.

She gave me another envelope and asked me to please deliver this one to Faith.

I go, "Who?"

And she goes, "The girl with spiky red hair in our American Government class."

And I looked around, because mostly everyone was gone.

"Maybe tomorrow morning?" she said. "As long as it's before third hour."

I go, "Is this one going to be mad, too?"

And she looked up and gave me a smile and I remembered that it changed her whole face last time and now it did, too. I don't think all smiles do that. But maybe I just never noticed.

She told me she'd asked lots of kids to be witnesses, but no one wanted to, so she was subpoenaing one. "It's like a court order to appear," she said. "Faith will have no choice."

"So, you're sayin' yeah, she's gonna be plenty mad," I said.

And she answered, "I don't think she'll be armed." And she smiled another one of those smiles. Her teeth line up just like corn. I don't mean they are yellow, or too small, I just mean . . .

Anyway, she got all embarrassed and looked back down at the floor and said, "Okay, so, her name's Faith."

And I said, "Got it."

DARIA

Until now, I'd always been sure of two places to hide and heal. One was within the pages of fiction, and the other was in sleep. There was a time when simply holding a novel in my hand and running my finger down its spine would calm me. And to sleep, all I had to do was lie on my side and hug my pillow.

Not anymore.

The first to go was literature. Suddenly, I was unable to concentrate on anything outside of the clicking and wheezing of my own fear. I found myself reading the same paragraph again and again, with no idea what I'd read. I even tried shaking my head clear, but nothing helped.

I closed the book and went to bed, but there was no peace to be found there, either. I must've woken up ten times, my psyche selecting from a bakery box of assorted trial-related horrors. I thought of pulling on some clothes and heading outside, maybe to lie in the hammock, but I got as far as unlocking two of the three locks on the back door, when suddenly all I could picture out there were waxy black widow spiders and silent packs of coyotes studying me with unblinking yellow eyes.

I knew the night had brought me peace not long ago, but now that just seemed crazy. Like juggling rattlesnakes for relaxation.

I crept back to my hot, airless room but my bed felt wrong. I dragged my pillow to the couch next, then contemplated sleeping in the bathtub.

Eventually morning came, with the sounds of my brothers and parents crashing around in their rooms. I considered staying home. It wouldn't be a lie to say that I was sick. But the good-girl habit is hard to break.

TUESDAY
Trial Resumes

CAMERON

I totally forgot about the envelope until the next day. I saw Red Spikes in first hour and it came back to me. I dug out the envelope, a little ragged from being in my pack, and I went up to the hair and said, "Faith?"

She looked shocked, I guess because I knew her name or was talking to her or like that. She nodded, and I gave her the envelope and sat back down.

I was behind her and couldn't see her face when she opened it, but I watched her back dissolve like cereal in milk.

Then it was third hour and I put it together that the quiet girl with the corn-smile who kept giving me envelopes was the same one the teacher was always ragging on to talk louder. She was the lawyer for the girl who got teased. And this red-spiked kid now had to go up in front of everyone, and boy, did she not want to.

As she was being sworn in, the redhead spied me across the room and gave me the hate-eye. I think maybe I'll cross *process server* off my list of future career possibilities.

MARCO

Gold started class by looking straight at *me* and saying she was going to change her phone number if the calls didn't stop. Dream on, witch. It wasn't me.

We moved our chairs and got in our courtroom places, while Gold went over to the white board and wrote, "Eggshell head doctrine." I figured if she wrote it on the board, it'd probably show up on a test, so I copied it down. Then she said, "Let's say you bop a guy on the head. Not so hard that it would do anything to a regular person, but in this case the guy's head cracks wide open, his brains spill out, and he dies."

Shannon and a few other kids go, "Eeew, gross," et cetera.

Gold continued, "Now you're arrested for murder and you go, 'Hey! Wait a minute! That tiny bop wouldn't have bothered a normal guy. It's not my fault the guy's skull was like an eggshell.'

"And that makes perfect sense, except for one thing: You're wrong. The law says, Too bad for you, Bud. You take your plaintiff where you find him. Whether his head is reinforced concrete or eggshells doesn't matter. You bopped him, he died; therefore, you killed him and you're outta luck, period."

I planned to ask my dad later, see if he remembered hearing anything in law school about shell-heads. Sounded weird to me, kinda sneaky. But as far as Ivy's skull, I'm not so sure any of us could take as much hammering as she had before we'd shatter. Everybody has got a breaking point somewhere, don't they? Maybe guys go Columbine and girls sue.

But I find it hard to believe that this is really going to be on our final exam, don't you? I think the whole eggshell thing is probably Gold's way of telling us not to listen to Owen's noise. As if I would.

I wasn't sure, though, if the other kids on the jury, besides old Wayne, knew what a dick Owen was. Kyle is pretty dim, and I sure wouldn't want Shannon on any jury of mine. Jennifer Puig is always scribbling in a black notebook—a journal or sketchbook or whatever—so I don't know how much she's paying attention, and the other two kids are total unknowns.

Gold claims it's our right as Americans to be judged by a jury of our peers. But my peers are total idiots! I swear, it creeps me out just thinking about these clowns deciding *my* fate.

Wayne Martin is deeply peculiar, in my opinion, but of all the jurors, he's the only one—besides myself—I'd trust not to vote on pure popularity.

Well, *popularity* is the wrong word. Popularity means everyone likes you. But no one likes our popular girls; it's more about *fear*. The word for them is *powerful* more than *popular*. Think soulless zombies; think living dead, hungry for fresh blood. If anything, I bet my fellow jurors were afraid they'd become the Anns' next victims if they got caught sympathizing with Ivy.

If I weren't on the jury, I'd take the witness stand. Or maybe I only *think* I would—because I can't or because I don't have to. I hate to think I'd be scared to speak out against the Anns of the world, like everybody else seems to be.

Gold wrote *burden of proof* on the board, so I copied that down too, even though I already knew what it meant. It meant Ann was right; she and Owen didn't have to prove diddly. It was entirely up to Ivy and Einstein to prove that Ann and her sidekicks bullied Ivy. That meant it was really up to Einstein, since Ivy was so spaced out.

But Einstein didn't have to convince every one of us. Not like in a criminal trial, where all twelve jurors have to be convinced *beyond a reasonable doubt.* Einstein only had to get four of us to be a little more than half sure that Ann and them might've been sorta mean to Ivy. "Fifty percent and a feather," Gold said. I admit I like that expression, even if it is Gold who said it.

Actually, that was one of the few civil phrases I like. Most of the good stuff goes with criminal cases. Like that perps are *guilty,* not *liable.* And they rot in prison or break rocks on a chain gang, instead of just having to fork over some cash. The only cool part of a civil case is that, if the bad guy has to cough up, the money goes straight into the pocket of the guy he screwed over, instead of the fine going to the state.

But Ivy didn't even stand to make a few bucks off this. All Einstein was asking for was an apology from the Anns, and for them to leave Ivy alone. Doesn't this seem like a lot of hassle for a stinking apology? Not that I was dying to get back to our usual classwork, but still.

ANN

While Ms. G went off about some really lame egg-thing that made absolutely *zero* sense, I watched Marco. He looked in every direction but mine—at the clock, the floor, out the window. And he looks at everyone, I swear, but me! What's up with *that*?

Meanwhile, Einstein whispered—as loud as she could—that she wanted Faith to take the stand.

Owen Uber Dweeb freaked right out of his banana tree.

I hissed at him, but he shrugged me off and hollered, "I object!"

Jeremy pounded his poor desk—we're all waiting for it to bust to toothpicks.

Ms. G asked Owen why he objected, and he said, "She didn't say anything to *me* about Faith!"

And Ms. G said, "Correct!" as if Owen had guessed the secret word and won the prize. Then she scurried, in her imitation Prada pumps, to the board and wrote, *NO TRIAL BY AMBUSH*.

"In a civil case," she said, "as I'm sure you all know from reading chapter thirty-two, you can bring no surprise witnesses. Everyone's entitled to clear and open access to all the pertinent information. Daria, your opponent has to have a chance to prepare for each witness."

Einstein looked like she'd been slammed in the face with a two-by-four. I'd never heard of this ambush thing, but *mu-ah-ha-ha!* get this: *Einstein hadn't either!* Ha! Miss Smarty All A's was not used to screwing up!

But Ms. G took pity on her, *of course*, and said that if none of us defendants had any objections, then Einstein could proceed with Faith.

I said it was fine with me. And Soph wasn't there. Did I already tell you that Sophie was absent? Well, she was, and I didn't know if she was sick or faking or what, till later, when we called her on Beni's cell. But we'll get to that. First, let me finish with the day's court happenings.

I told Ms. Gold I was fine with Faith taking the stand. And like I said, Sophie wasn't there—not that she was there even when she *was* there, now that she was a chair.

That left Beni, and she suddenly seemed to be letting idiotic *Owen* make all her decisions! I don't know why she didn't fire him when I did, but I was beginning to suspect that it was one of two things: Either Benita had the hots for him, which was enough right there to make me lose my lunch, especially since she *knows* what I went through with him last year. Or, possibility number two, she was a *total* wimp and had lost her mind, which is not such a stretch.

Whichever reason, Owen finally quit his grumbling and said it was okay with him and Benita that Faith take the stand. So she did. And it was *brilliant*.

DARIA

I could understand Faith's being angry, but I had to get *someone* to go up there. And I wasn't asking her to do or say anything so terrible, simply tell the truth. That's all.

Faith had said she'd think about it. Then she avoided me the rest of the day and didn't return my calls that night. So what could I do? Everyone else I'd asked had brushed me off with a flat-out *no*. Faith was the only one who even agreed to give it some thought. And actually, I figured that if I had Cameron subpoena her, everyone would know it wasn't her own choice to give evidence and no one could blame her. I thought she'd be grateful to be *made* to do the right thing.

So I wasn't all that surprised that Faith snarled at me as she took the stand. I thought she was simply showing everyone that she was there against her will. I was nervous, sure, but it didn't make me any extra nervous that Faith smirked at Ann while Ms. Gold was swearing her in. I just sat there, suspecting nothing.

Jeremy asked Bryce if the tape recorder was on. Then he asked him a second time, to be funny. Then he asked Bryce if there was a tape in there, and he offered to give him an extra second to check, which was mean, but everyone laughed.

Then Jeremy had Faith state her name and then it was my turn.

I peeked at Cameron and saw that he was awake. Knowing he was watching gave me an added jolt of panic. Not what I needed.

The night before, I'd asked Ivy whether she wanted me

to have Faith describe the gritty details of the torture she'd witnessed, or just stick to a basic overview. I assumed Ivy would find it unbearable if we went all the way into it, but no, Ivy didn't seem to get humiliated. Perhaps she'd had embarrassment hammered out of her by Ann, Benita, and Sophie's daily attacks. Or perhaps she was born without the shame gene. That would be nice. But weird.

Accepting that Ivy meant what she'd said, I intended to ask Faith to be specific about the things she'd seen. I knew the answers would make everyone cringe, but I assumed the discomfort would act to bring the whole nightmare to a quick end.

I planned to ask Faith to talk about one time in particular. It was in our cabin, one night on our sixth-grade camping retreat. Faith and I were semi-friends back then, and we'd been sitting on my cot, playing cards. I remember the entire scene perfectly, and I knew Faith had to remember it too. It was more or less unforgettable.

I clutched my list of questions and stood facing Faith in the witness stand. The first question on my list was meant simply as a warm-up. I read it aloud: "Have you ever seen any of the codefendants being mean to my client?"

"Maybe that one," Faith answered, pointing to the empty chair.

"Sophie?" I asked.

"No," Faith giggled. "The chair!" The entire class cracked up, so I tried to smile too.

Then, starting over, I said, "Faith, have you ever seen Ann, Benita, or Sophie tease Ivy?"

And Faith answered, "No." Just like that. She simply opened her mouth and lied. It knocked the breath right out of my chest, and to tell you the truth, I have no idea what I did next. The room whirled.

Although this wasn't a real court, it stunned me that Faith would lie. That possibility had never really occurred to me. I know that Shannon had recently lied pretty much the same way, so perhaps my shock illustrates only what a slow learner I am. But Shannon had always been shallow and mean-spirited, whereas Faith had appeared to have a heart—at least enough heart to do the right thing if *forced* to. I'd simply assumed that if I asked her flat out . . .

Well, it obviously didn't matter what I thought. I was wrong. About everything. My list of questions was useless. I'm not sure how long I stood there like a fool, with the room spinning and no one saying anything.

Ultimately, I managed to say something like, "Think back to the camp retreat in sixth grade. We were sitting on my cot, playing hearts. The deck of cards had ships on the back. You'd brought them back from your cruise to Ensenada. Remember?"

"You're under oath," I reminded her. But she rolled her eyes. I guess an oath taken on a textbook doesn't stand for much.

Then I'm afraid I started to babble and stutter. I don't know precisely what I asked Faith after that, but I do know that she lied smoothly, calmly, as if it was no big deal. Finally, I gave up and said, "I have no further questions," and sat down in misery.

ANN

Shows a person's just got to have *faith*! Tee-hee! Get it?

But *seriously,* when Faith first dragged her wide load up to the witness chair, I thought, "Oh, no! She's gonna totally cave." Because right before class, when she told me she'd been ordered to appear, I figured . . . Well, I don't know what I figured, except, This totally sucks! It was great that she told me, though. What if she hadn't?

And now I'm so nice to her, it would make you *gag*. Nice, nice, *nice*! And up there on the hot seat, Faith was nicey-nice back at me, and it went great. See? It's like they always said: "Do unto others as you'd like them to do unto you!"

I knew that Beni and I were going to have to eat lunch with Faith and Shannon for days, but everything has its price—the justice system at work.

Meanwhile, Marco was nodding away over in the jury box. Whether he was nodding in agreement or bobbing to some inner tunes, I didn't know. I never know what's going on in that *gorgeous* head of his. He's so *deep*! He knows stuff about natives and primitives and all that, and it gives me shivers to picture him, you know, sitting around a fire, wearing a tiny scrap of, like, buffalo hide or whatever, and chanting and sweating and being all *tribal*. . . .

Where were we?

Oh, yeah. The court thingy.

Well, so Owen got up and asked Faith if anyone *paid* her for her testimony. She acted offended and answered truthfully, "*No!* Of course not!" I don't know what all he was getting at, exactly, but Faith put him in his place with a *look*.

I would've flipped him off, but Ms. Gold was right there.

She's weird—Ms. Gold, that is. I never really noticed *how* weird till this trial. She's *so* into it, it's practically sick. Maybe she wants to go to law school or whatever. Trying to figure out what makes teachers tick is a dead end.

Anyway, you'd think Owen would've been psyched that Einstein practically *handed* him a winning case by putting Faith up there, but it put his knickers in a total twist. Leave it to a toad like Owen Anderson to *complain* that Einstein was making this too easy for him.

All I've got to say is, thank God he's not my lawyer!

MARCO

Faith lied like a pro. It was almost impressive, in a sickening sort of way.

I'm reminded of a story my dad told me a while back about how you catch wolves. Want to hear it? Well, according to him, you stick a knife in the ground with the blade facing up, and you smear a little blood on it. That's all.

When a wolf comes along and smells the blood, he'll lick the knife and cut his tongue. That'll make his tongue bleed, and he'll like the taste, so he'll lick the knife again. And again. Then the other wolves smell blood. . . .

Anyhow, after Faith's performance, it was Owen's turn to call a witness. You could tell from looking at Benita that Owen hadn't talked this over with her. She and Ann were as surprised as the rest of us when Owen asked Gold to take the stand.

Jeremy got a huge kick out of telling her to state her full name.

Gold said her first name was Linda, and her middle initial was *S*. I guess even adults can hate their middle names. I bet it's Sue. Half the women her age are named Susan, including my mom and a bunch of her friends.

Gold swore to tell the truth and sat in the hot seat.

Benita got the giggles.

Then Owen, looking hugely proud of himself, asked Gold if she was ever picked on in middle school, and she said yes.

He asked if she'd picked on other kids, and she said, "I don't remember picking on anyone, no."

And he said, "But you might have?"

Gold said, "I suppose it's possible."

Owen smirked. He asked how long she'd been teaching, and she said, "Seven years."

"And have you ever seen any students pick on any other students in that time?" he asked.

Gold said, "That's very clever, Owen. But it's not relevant. Just because something happens, even if it happens a lot, that doesn't make it okay." She started to get up, but Jeremy banged his desk and said, "Answer the question, Linda S."

Gold flicked a look at him, like maybe she'd have him dethroned, but you could see her deciding to let it slide. She sat back down and said, "Yes. I have seen many bullies over the years."

"So you're saying that in your experience, school is a cruel place and Benita and Sophie didn't do anything really unusual; that is, nothing any worse than is expected here, correct?"

Now Gold looked annoyed and said, "No. What I *said* was that no matter how often people do something wrong, it is still wrong."

Owen threw up his hands and said, "Thank you! I have no further questions!" as if he'd just won the match point.

Ann said she didn't have anything to ask this witness, which was smart, seeing as in the end, it's Gold who's going to grade us.

Einstein still looked so flipped out over Faith's lies that she sat there practically drooling on herself. Jeremy told Gold she was free to go, as if he'd been deciding whether or not to throw her in jail.

Gold brushed herself off and marched to the board on

her stumpy little legs. She wrote CLOSING STATEMENTS in giant letters. Then she said, "If no one has any further witnesses to call, then tomorrow we shall hear closing arguments." She nodded at Owen and Ann, then at Einstein, because she meant the three of them.

The bell rang and most everybody bolted for the door, except me. Well, a few people hung around talking to each other before leaving, but soon the room was emptied out. I couldn't manage to haul my bones up out of my seat. Gold shot a suspicious glance over her shoulder, like she thought I was staying behind to steal her chalk.

I was either getting sick or this trial was really getting to me. I didn't know which was worse—to be paralyzed by depression or suddenly flattened by some disease.

It took effort to hoist myself to my feet. My dad probably felt heavy and immovable like that all the time, whether he was depressed or not. That must really suck.

CAMERON

That quiet girl who kept giving me envelopes looked like
the redhead had run over her dog. Poor kid. You could see
she was blown away, like her whole world had gone bad.
Maybe it had.

I know that low feeling when someone turns out not to
be who you thought. It makes you think you probably got
everything else wrong too. Like the world isn't the friendly blue-and-green planet you'd thought it was, but just a
cold, ugly rock swarming with maggots.

I must'a fallen asleep then or just zoned out. But after
the bell, I saw she still looked trashed. I followed her out
the door and said, "Got any envelopes you want me to
deliver?"

But she shook her head, all doom and gloom. It was
enough to break your heart, her standing there like that,
sad to the bone. So I go, "You're looking for someone to say
they saw Ann and them picking on Poison Ivy, is that it?"

And she nodded.

So I say, "Well, I seen it. Lotsa times. You want me to say
so?"

And she gets all surprised, and looks at me like I'm
something amazing. "You'd do that?" she says.

So I shrug, and I'm all, "Well, sure. Why not? It's not
like I'd be lying or anything."

And she smiled a little at me and said, "Really? You'd go
up in front of everyone and say that you saw those girls be
mean?"

And again I go, "Well, it's the truth."

Then she was smiling all over the place, she was *that*

happy. And I'm thinking, This is one strange chick. But her smile made me smile back, and we stood there showing each other our teeth until she said she needed to get to her next class. And I'm thinking, I gotta find out this girl's *name*.

ANN

Since Soph didn't show up at school, we called her at lunch. I could hear only Beni's side of the conversation. "You sick?"—short listen—"Well, so, how come you're not here?"

Then there was a longer pause while Beni's eyes got huge and she started shrieking, "You're kidding! You're totally kidding! Omigod! I mean, seriously? I can't believe it!"

The bottom line is: Soph's *leaving*! There was some stuff about her dad and Ms. Broccoli, but Beni was funky on details. The important part is that Sophie's out of here for good! Not moving away, but transferring to private school because her parents think her *reputation* here has been *destroyed*!

What reputation would *that* be? Her reputation as the kid who can blow the biggest smoke rings in Sea View? Or her reputation as the girl most likely to get VD by junior year?

Freakiest of all, Beni says Soph's out-of-her-mind bummed over the whole thing! She suddenly *loves* this dump, although we all, including her, have only hated every single second of every single day since school started. I do not get it. She's finally going, and she doesn't *want* to go?

Beni kept saying, "Can you believe it?" I couldn't quit repeating, "*Reputation*? Sophie's *reputation*?" Then we had screaming, giggling seizures for, like, an hour, although we'll probably miss Soph to tears later.

IVY

The giant yellow sharks don't have to swerve and dive, because we swim right into their jaws. I'm fated to feed myself each day to bus number 43, which heads east like the smog. Others swim down other throats and are digested along other routes. I was mistakenly swallowed by the number 14 once, so I can testify that it winds its way uphill and excretes gradually—one passenger at a time along a twisty tunnel of trees and tall gates.

Number 43 doesn't go in for those delicate deposits. He squirts us out in great gobs, a dozen kids in one grunt on Brand near the police station. Then farther east, at the south projects. The last blast includes me.

But it's all good. As a jellyfish, I have a perfect, and perfectly luminescent, bubble within a bubble. At its very center, I breathe only the purest, sweetest air. The sounds and fumes and slurs and stares, the dust and rust, are all deflected, reflected by my shiny, soapy surface.

I'm spared the churning of number 43's guts. His digestive juices cannot dissolve me. I ride. I glide. Safe inside.

Others thrash and tumble with the uneven road and the faulty shocks and the creaking seats, while I float and gloat. But they aren't envious because they don't see me.

Ask Faith. She never saw me being tortured, and she can't see me now.

Faith? Do you see me?

No answer. She can't hear the question over her own screams. She's being jostled and jolted—devoured and digested.

TUESDAY NIGHT
Adjournment

DARIA

Mom said it's too bad I'm underage, because a drink would do me a world of good. (She was having a glass of wine.) I'd been telling her about my day in court, and she thought the whole story was hilarious.

"I think it's valuable to be learning about corruption and deceit. Great preparation for the real world," she laughed.

There's no talking to my mom when she's like that. She wasn't falling down, slobbering drunk, she was simply in that "it's all a lark" mood where she finds my problems amusing. To be fair, it's not my life in particular that's nonsensical; my dad's and my brothers' are also, and her own, too. She told me once that she had to keep laughing or she'd cry. And that if she took any of it seriously, she'd go mad.

"But don't be too hard on that girl whatsername," Mom said.

"Faith?"

"Yeah, Faith. Ironic name, eh?" Here my mother giggled and refilled her glass.

"I'm not being hard on her. I'm simply disappointed," I said.

"Yes," Mom said. "But you know what?"

"What?"

"I bet she didn't know she was going to lie until she opened her mouth, and out it came."

"So? What difference does it make if it was planned or not? It was a big, fat *lie*!"

"It matters with murder," Mom said. "Impulsive or premeditated. Planned or a crime of passion. Maybe this was a *lie* of passion."

That's what I mean about there being no talking to her at times like that.

I went to my room and stared into my closet, trying to decide what to wear tomorrow. What I *wanted* was a huge, hooded, floor-length cloak that would turn me invisible. Barring that, however, I didn't have time to worry about costuming. I had homework piling up like freight cars in a wreck because I hadn't been able to think about anything but this awful trial.

I pulled my calculus book out of my backpack, but then I remembered Cameron's big face smiling down at me, and it propelled me right back to my closet, searching for something to wear tomorrow.

But that was silly. I knew it would be ridiculous to let myself have a crush on Cameron. Boys like him are from a whole different solar system than girls like me. But there was no getting around how sweet his smile was and how amazingly sweet it was of him to offer to be my witness.

Then my insides went cold. Tomorrow—more horror, with Ivy chewing on her mucus and gazing blankly at nothing. And Ms. Gold harping at me to talk louder: "Daria, dear, can you *speak up,* please?"

And me wanting to yell until it shook the ceiling tiles. Wanting to holler until the walls cracked and the ground rumbled: *"No! I cannot speak louder, because if I do, it will be to scream that I hate you! Hate you! Hate you! and wish you and your evil trial would go straight to hell!"* Sigh.

Dread is so physical.

I've heard of normal-sized people discovering they had tumors as big as footballs in their intestines. It always made me wonder how they carried a football-sized *anything* in there without noticing. Where did their other organs go to make room for it?

But now I understand. I had a football-sized dread in my gut and it squeezed everything else out of its way. My liver cowered at the sight of it. My kidneys clenched like fists, covering their eyes, trying to avoid contact.

If you've never felt it, I don't expect you to understand how deeply I dreaded returning to class. Dreaded being back in front of everyone, feeling too tall, too wide, too visible, like a huge target, all alone.

But wait! This time I wouldn't be as alone! Cameron would be up there with me! I felt the tumorous dread shrivel, collapsing in on itself as it shrank. For a moment, I could actually breathe.

Then I remembered that I wasn't supposed to bring surprise witnesses.

Uh-oh. Should I call Ms. Gold? I really, *really* didn't want to, but she'd made it perfectly clear that I wasn't supposed to spring witnesses on anyone. "No ambushing your opponent," she'd said, surprised that I hadn't already known that.

But she also said she wished she'd never given out her home phone number because she was being inundated with calls.

Oh, no! I'd have to call Owen so he could prepare his cross-examination. Worse, I'd also have to call Ann, since she was acting as her own lawyer.

The mass of dread re-formed, pressing up, up against my lungs. I took shallow half breaths. I knew in my twisted gut that my mom was wrong about Faith's deciding on the spur of the moment to lie. I felt sure that Ann or Benita or Sophie or all of them together had gotten to her.

Would they get to Cameron, too? Had they already?

Cameron was sweet but was he even awake enough to know what was really going on here? What if he mentioned to Ann and the others that he was going to take the stand tomorrow? After all, he was friends with them, whereas I was just some stranger. He didn't owe me any loyalty.

Then the realization hit with a thud between my ribs— Cameron was probably on their side all along! I felt dizzy, and sweat burst out of every pore. Of course he'd been teasing me, laughing at me. They all were!

How could I have been so stupid? How could I have actually thought a guy like *him* could smile like *that* at me, and mean it? How could I have fallen for such an obvious trick?

And what had made me think Cameron was so sweet in the first place? I'd barely exchanged ten words with the guy. He never said anything in class that would indicate sweetness. I'd simply made him up. Created my own sweet Frankenstein's monster in a pathetic loner's fantasy based on nothing but my own breathtaking loneliness.

I was so stupid. So sickeningly stupid and gullible.

Then I remembered Jennifer Puig's horrible Web site, and suddenly my brain began to hum in a haze of swarming cyber gnats. Buzzing, biting insults, *frigid, cold.* The disembodied sting of sneering laughter. Everyone smirking online, Cameron among them.

How could I face him, or any of them, ever again?

WAYNE MARTIN
Blog Entry

Our third-hour Government class has made a mockery of the American judicial system from end to end.

For our system to succeed, it requires the best and truest efforts of each and every participant—an open-minded, unbiased jury; an impartial judge; learned counsel; and honest and forthright witnesses. Therefore, in light of the fact that, in the vast majority of cases in this country, it is our great fortune that justice IS admirably served, we can take heart from concluding that most people ARE good.

Why Ms. Gold's third-hour American Government class so misrepresents the true nature of our citizenry, I cannot guess! What convergence of stars and planets? What combination of ethers and ice brought together such a flawed assemblage?

Conceivably it is akin to the infection-like formation of terrorist cells or racist cults or wrong-minded fraternities within an otherwise healthy society. Rare, in a political system as strong as ours, but not unheard of. A warning! An important reminder to be ever vigilant! To stay alert against buffoonery! Take nothing for granted!

WEDNESDAY
Closing Statements

BRYCE—Court Reporter and Bookmaker

I figure, dude, why not make a little spare change on the side? A buck a bet won't kill anyone. All's I had to do was explain that *liable* was civil for *guilty,* and they swarmed like flies. I'd only been at it since first hour and already the pot was at eighteen and mounting by the second. Even kids who weren't in my government class were coughing up on this one.

My dad was right—going to school *does* help a guy's career!

ANN

I'm giving my black jeans a second chance and wearing my favorite purple top. It's picture day. I'd almost forgotten because of all that trial stuff and the news that Soph's changing schools. She's so spoiled. Can you believe her *da* is pulling her out and *paying* to send her to an entirely different school just because of this stupid trial?

Bryce, who is only the biggest loser this side of the Rockies, was taking *bets* on whether I'm going to win the case. I plunked down my buck, and he went, "One liable or not liable?"

I'm all, "Well, *du-uh!*"

And he goes, "Sorry, 'duh' is not a choice, it's either liable or not." And just when I was about to take back my money and call him all the names he deserved to be called, I hear a laugh behind me, and who was it? *Marco*, of course.

It wasn't an "I hate your guts and think you are an ugly troll" laugh. But it wasn't an "I love you madly, let's run off and smooch under the bleachers" laugh, either.

I tried to flirt him up a little, made a few cracks about Bryce the Bookie and the betting and stuff, but nothing. Zip. Zilch. Nada. That makes *two* strikes against my black jeans. And it's *no fair*! He's so completely gorgeous.

After first hour, I saw Einstein creeping down the edge of the hall, clinging to the lockers. She looked even worse than usual. Eyes sunken like a strung-out junkie, scraggly-haired, shoulders hunched. Not very lawyerly. Especially not very *winningly* lawyerly.

Not that I'm complaining, but when you get right down to it, it's *Einstein* that's killing Poison Ivy, not me. Einstein's got *no* case, *no* witnesses, no *nothing*. If I were The Weed, I'd sue *her*! Hee-hee!

Tomorrow I'm raising my bet to five bucks!

MARCO

Bryce was working out of his locker, which was near mine. It was amazing how many kids showed up waving their lunch money. Leave it to Bryce to find a way to cash in on this trial. Don't get me wrong, I like Bryce fine. He's only a different kind of guy, jumpy and quick and always working some angle.

Anyhow, I was just hanging, watching the zoo, when Ann showed up, changing the entire atmosphere of the hall. I'm serious; it's like the chemical composition of the air, the ions or whatever, line up differently around her. It makes me stupid. Especially since she was wearing one of those miniature shirts with all this smooth, incredibly touchable-looking skin showing under it. I knew I could easily span her tiny waist with one hand. This hand. The one that started reaching for her with a will of its own. It could seem like an accident. Like I just slipped, hit a bump . . .

But with great effort, I managed to reroute my sweaty paw and make it push my glasses up my greasy beak instead, just in time to see her place a bet on her own innocence. That snapped me out of my trance. How could she do that? Was it possible Ann really didn't think she'd treated Ivy badly? How nuts was this girl?

Then, as if she'd read my mind, Ann spun around and asked me if I'd bet for or against her. I was no match for her head-on smile and the way she looks at a person like you were the center of the universe. Boom. I was instantly back in Tlingit-babble mode. This time, I said something lame like, "I don't think it would be kosher for me to bet since I'm on the jury and have to remain impartial." Then I kicked myself for acting like such an uptight wuss. Then kicked myself again, for caring.

"*Shannon* bet on me, and *she*'s on the jury," Ann said in a teasing voice that reduced what was left of my brain to goo. God knows what stupid thing I said next.

Then, luckily, the bell rang, and in a whirl of hair, Ann disappeared.

Phew!

Einstein was late to third hour and looked like she'd been up puking all night. Gold asked her and Owen and Ann if any of them had any further evidence to present or witnesses to call, and they all said no. Gold pointed to the words CLOSING ARGUMENTS on the board and said these were a way for the sides to review their strongest points for the jury.

"As if either side had any strong points," Wayne Martin mumbled beside me in the jury box.

Einstein shuffled up, with her eyes on the floor, and spoke so quietly that I can't absolutely swear to what she said, but I think it was, "The codefendants intentionally inflicted emotional distress on my client and we all know it." And something like, "Vote your conscience."

"Now we're a jury of conscience?" Wayne muttered, a little louder this time. I looked at him and discovered that he'd been talking to *me*.

Next, Owen got up and strutted back and forth, saying, "Ladies and gentlemen of the jury, Benita is a normal kid, and she acted like a normal kid. Not like an angel, maybe, but not like a monster, either. She never hit Ivy or tripped or kicked or shot or bit or stabbed or poisoned her. And she never threatened to, either."

Benita was giggling for a change.

"Sophie, however," Owen continued, pointing at her chair, which *still* cracked some kids up, "may possibly have said a few thoughtless things, although we heard *no* witnesses and were shown *no* evidence that she did. But let's say, just to be open-minded, that sometimes Sophie may have said things to or about Ivy that weren't all that nice. Well, my question is, So what? Isn't freedom of speech one of the main things we're so proud of in this great land of ours?"

Owen looked at us as if waiting for an answer. Some of my fellow jurors nodded back at him—and not only Shannon.

Satisfied, Owen went on to say, "So, I, too, say vote your conscience. And find Benita and Sophie not liable."

Wayne Martin put his head in his hands and groaned.

Ann got up next and said, "Noble jury and distinguished judge," which made Jeremy stand up and bow. "Sophie is switching to another school. Why? Because Ivy brought this case against her and embarrassed her so totally that her dad thinks her entire life here is *ruined*. Now she's got to start all over somewhere new, where no one knows her and she hasn't got a single friend. I, for one, would call *that* the intentional infliction of emotional distress. But that doesn't mean I'm going to turn around and *sue* Ivy for traumatizing one of my best friends and driving her out of school! And that's not even the point.

"The point is, I told Ivy and her lawyer to *prove* that I was mean to Ivy, and they didn't even come close! I ask you to consider the facts, and the facts are *there are no facts*! Not one!"

She was right. Ivy's side hadn't come up with any proof.

But just because Ann wasn't dumb or because she looked like some love goddess didn't change how cold and heartless she was inside. At least that's what I kept telling myself. Nonetheless, when Ann turned to sit back down, I felt a wave of that drunken fog again. Life is mysterious, no doubt about it.

Gold scurried to the board to write something, but Cameron raised his big old hand and said, "Uh, Miss Teacher?"

She turned around and said, "Yes, Cameron? Have a nice nap?" in that same snotty tone that she usually saves for me.

Everybody had a little laugh because it's true, Cam sleeps through a lot of class. He looked sheepish, but he went on to say, "I thought I was going to be a whatever you call it. Get up and say what I saw?"

Gold tilted her head like a dog hearing a funny sound.

Cameron pointed at Einstein. "She was gonna, you know, call on me or like that."

Einstein, pale as death, was burning holes in the floor with her eyes.

Gold was confused. "You were going to be a witness?" she asked.

Cameron nodded.

"It's a little late now," she said. "You snooze, you lose. Unless . . . Daria, do you have anything to add?"

Einstein went even paler, if that's possible, and slunk lower in her seat. She shook her head without lifting her eyes.

Next to me, Wayne grumbled, "Add to what? She never

presented any case in the first place!" The disgust in his voice was chilling. I looked at him and he said, "Ineffective assistance of counsel. Easily grounds for legal malpractice.
fact, we should move for a mistrial. The counsel did

"When I was a kid," Cameron said, "there was this story about a president or a king or something who walked around with nothing on, but everyone pretended they could see fancy clothes on him because they thought only losers and misfits couldn't see his cool threads. And that's what's happening here. No one's saying nothing about how mean those girls were to Poison Ivy, even though everybody knows they're butt-naked."

I practically shot up out of my chair to give Cam a standing ovation. I didn't, but I gotta tell you, I loved that speech, and I wasn't the only one who went nuts. Kids were all over the place, laughing and what not, with the Anns shrieking hysterically and Jeremy walloping his desk for a change, chanting, "Off with their heads! Off with *all* their heads!"

Even Wayne Martin tipped his chair back and crossed his arms over his chest, looking pleased. I guess he, too, was a sucker for a happy ending.

Meanwhile, I watched Einstein drag her eyeballs off the floor to look into Cam's big old face, and crack a smile. I don't think I'd ever seen Einstein smile before. I didn't know she could. If I didn't know better, I'd think, from the way they were grinning at each other, that there was something going on between those two.

I shook my head in amazement—it had played perfectly! Just when it had looked so bleak and hopeless, in rode Prince Charming to save the day. Like any noble knight worth his beans, Cam exposed the evil wrongdoers and whisked Daria-in-distress to safety, in the nick of time!

I never would've pegged Daria for the damsel or Cam for the hero, but sure! He's perfect for the role. Big bear of a guy with a heart of gold and no need to prove himself. Honest and true and all the other corny, fairy-tale, super-hero clichés.

I loved it. It was enough to restore a cynic's hope and make a guy feel all right with the world! Yes sir, justice done.

Chaos reigned until the bell.

I don't know about anyone else, but I couldn't stop smiling the rest of the day. The jury still had to rule, so the whole thing wasn't really done yet, but still, the relief was awesome. It made me realize how wound up this trial had been making me. I couldn't wait to tell my dad.

"A *gambling* pool? Here? In class?" Her amazement now looks like the genuine article, and dude, I wish I'd kept mum. Here's something a guy's gotta keep in mind: Just because a teacher's short doesn't mean she's any less of a *teacher,* if you know what I mean.

So I dumped the tapes on her desk and split.

THURSDAY
Jury Deliberation

MARCO

Someone must've tipped Gold off about Bryce, because she started class with a lecture about gambling that ended with her saying it was wrong to, quote, *profit by other people's misfortune*, unquote.

Whose misfortune did she mean? Ivy's? For being vivisected by the class? Wouldn't Gold herself be the one to blame for that? Obviously, this trial was *her* baby. At first I'd thought maybe it was Ivy's idea, but one look at her picking fleas off herself had convinced me that this had not been her brainchild, if, in fact, Ivy *had* a brain.

I was way past thinking Gold might be doing this to help. Her interest in Ivy's well-being was clearly nil. I no longer even thought it was Gold trying to get her name in the paper for hot-shot teaching recognition or whatever. But if you're waiting for me to come up with a legitimate explanation for Gold's motive, you're wasting your time. Far as I could tell, she was just a certifiable psychopath who enjoyed watching kids squirm.

Anyhow, after her gambling rant, Gold turned her back on the rest of the class and zeroed in on us in the jury. She repeated that we should consider the evidence and *only* the evidence in coming up with our decision. And each time, I swear she glowered at me like I was the one who was going to screw everything up.

Then, as if we were brain-dead, she repeated that four out of the six of us only had to be a feather more than half convinced one way or the other. That's it. Oh, and she told us that no one was allowed *not* to vote. She said there had to be six votes, but only four of us had to agree.

It couldn't have seemed simpler. How hard could it be for four of us to agree that we were semi-sure that the Anns might've been mean to Ivy sometimes. Piece of cake.

Then Gold had us put our names in a bag to draw for the alternate. I'd forgotten that one of us was going to be cut from the jury. I hoped it was me, and I hoped it wasn't.

Gold drew Wayne Martin's name, and from the look on his face, it was clear Wayne had not had mixed feelings. In fact, I've never seen him look so ticked. Not even when Owen tried to keep him off the jury in the first place. Well, Owen was sure to be happy now.

When I got up to leave with the rest of the jurors, Wayne saluted me as if we were soldiers in a war movie.

Gold herded the rest of us down the hall to the custodian's windowless hovel, which smelled like many putrid and foul things put together. We filed in and took seats on chairs and boxes. I sat on a white plastic barrel of that red sawdust Mr. Mark sprinkles on barf before he sweeps it up.

Gold stood in the open doorway and told us to start by selecting a foreperson, however we wanted to. Then she wished us luck, closed the heavy door, and was gone.

Kyle thought we should arm wrestle, but the rest of us decided to put our names on scraps again, and grab one. Then we had to argue endlessly over who was going to do the grabbing. I swear it took the entire class period to pick the damn foreperson. And after all that, it turned out to be Shannon, which was sick, considering the foreperson was supposed to keep it all going and she was too stupid to keep *gravity* going.

When the bell rang, barely audible through the closet door, everybody groaned, knowing we'd be back in there with the mops tomorrow. When my mom did jury duty, she got free parking and doughnuts. We didn't even get air to breathe. At least we weren't a *sequestered* jury, where they don't let you go home at night or see anyone but each other until you reach a verdict.

Gold caught us on the way out and said, "Remember, don't discuss this case with anyone over the next twenty-three hours." Then she looked straight at me and said, "Understand, *Marco*?" in that way that made me want to knock her head off her shoulders.

Out of nowhere, Ann came smiling up at me at lunch and said, "How goes it?"

I said, "Fine."

"*Fine* fine, or just *fine*?" she asked, as if it were all a joke.

I shrugged, and she said, "Oh, Marco! You take everything so *seriously*!" and she filled the air with her laugh and threw her hair in my direction.

Did she really think the whole thing was funny? She must know we were going to vote against her and she was going to lose. Didn't that bug her?

I looked around the lunchroom for a place to eat and saw Einstein, alone, with her nose in a book, as always. In the center of the room, Ann's people held a place for her. They waved frantically, all smiles. And way over there in the corner, sat Ivy, staring dimly into space. For one woozy second, the imbalance and shakiness of it all made me want to grab Ann's hair, twist it into a noose, and just *strangle* her with it.

Either that, or wrap it around myself like a cocoon.

BRYCE

Dude, it felt weird with our desks back in the plain old rows. Goldilocks gives us "jury instructions," which got nothing to do with me. Some stuff about feathers. I dunno. Then she takes those guys to the janitor's cell where they get to kick back while the rest of us suckers take a stinking quiz!

How fair is *that*?

Later, Cam catches me at the soda machine and we do this handshake that goes on forever. Says it was the thing in his old school. Then he goes, "Can I ask you something?"

And I go, "'Course, dude."

And he goes, "You know that girl with the real soft voice who was in the court play?"

I think for a second, then I go, "Yeah, what about her?"

Cameron gets all shy and stuff and goes, "I gotta ask you this, my friend . . . ," he says, "What's her name?"

I shake my head over a guy like him going for a chick like her. "Her name's Einstein," I say.

And Cam gets this fuzzy look in his eyes. Then, totally serious and dreamy, he goes, "Einstein. What a pretty name."

IVY

My mother called me into her bathroom. She was sitting on the edge of the bathtub in her robe, filing the calluses on her heels. She uses this big paddlelike file and the dead skin falls like snow. It is one of the single most disgusting images of my life. I dearly hope that on my deathbed, when my life flashes before my eyes, it will not include snaps of my mother filing her feet, or my father trimming his nose hairs, or for that matter, any single moment out of my life in school.

Come to think of it, there aren't all that many images I'd like to revisit, except maybe a few cartoons that made me laugh and a place I once snorkeled. All I can hope is that my flashing life will be mercifully short.

But that's not the issue now. What matters here is that my mom had obviously been mulling over the *name* business, and she wanted to clear the air. She started by asking me if I'd told my dad the part about Owen saying it was my parents' fault for naming me Ivy.

I said no. I didn't add that I hadn't mentioned *anything* to him about the trial.

My mother stopped her scraping to say, "Well, you should! *Ivy* was *his* idea. Feel free to remind him, next time you see him, that *I* wanted to name you Chloe!"

What was I supposed to say to that?

FRIDAY
The Verdict

MARCO

Back in the jury closet with the push brooms and bathroom sanitizer, I suggested we take a vote right off the bat to see how far we were from a decision. Then we had to squabble over *how* to take the vote.

Shannon said, "To hell with all that secretive crap. Let's just raise hands." Then everybody but me raised their hands for *not* liable.

"Cool!" Shannon said. "All's we needed was four, right? Didn't we just need four?"

A few kids nodded back at her.

"Awesome!" Shannon cheered. "We've got five! We won!"

Kyle gave a double thumbs-up. Partly because he'd do anything if he thought it would give him a chance with Shannon, and partly because he had the mind of a slug.

"But how about the fact that everybody here knows those girls treat Ivy like scum?" I asked.

Two kids looked at me blankly; a third, that girl Jennifer who thinks she's so Goth, got busy playing with her lip ring.

Shannon cracked her gum and said, "Since when are you so tight with Ivy?"

And Kyle, eager to impress Shannon, added, "It's not like I see *you* asking her out, Marco"—snicker—"unless there's something we don't know."

I ignored them and continued, "All Ivy's asking for is an apology and to be left alone. Seems to me she's got at least that much coming."

"Yeah, but Einstein didn't have any *proof*," Shannon said. "It's not about what we personally might think in private, it's about the trial! Remember? Ms. Gold only said that, like, twenty times."

I wondered if *this* is why my dad doesn't practice law.

I tried again. "What about Cameron's testimony and all the stuff he said?"

Jennifer Puig spoke up. "It's not like he was sworn in or anything. Cameron wasn't even a witness, really."

Kyle snorted. "Cam's a great guy, but you gotta admit, his elevator doesn't exactly reach the top floor."

Shannon laughed, shaking her head. "That rambling stuff about *The Emperor's New Clothes* . . . I don't know, is it *me* or was he, like, talking in his sleep?"

Kyle hooted over Shannon's brilliant wit, and added, "And Cam's *evidence,* if you can call it that, was way too late—the trial was, like, over."

My fellow jurors half smiled and forced a few laughs. To be fair, no one besides Shannon and Kyle seemed to be celebrating or considering this a great victory. The other kids even looked a little surprised at the outcome. But there it was: decided. Beauty wins and truth is irrelevant. Grim, isn't it?

Of course, they weren't doing anything wrong. The jury instructions were to base our votes on the evidence presented, and that's what they'd done. They'd followed orders.

I wished *anyone* other than Wayne Martin had been the alternate. Preferably Shannon, but any of the other sheep would have done. I was sure that if he were there, Wayne and I would've been able to sway at least one other vote, and that would've changed the verdict. Without Wayne, I had to do it myself, and I had to convince *two* people, not one.

I bet a couple of them were secretly on Ivy's side, even if

they didn't know it. And they probably wanted me to sway them and save them from themselves. They had to, didn't they? How else could they live with themselves? They must've hoped to be led away from the Shannons, rescued from their own small-mindedness. But I couldn't promise any of them safe passage. I couldn't guarantee that Ann and Benita's retaliation wouldn't be harsh. I could offer no protection from the revenge of the powerful.

So much for the fairy tale, and for how stupidly optimistic I'd been only the day before. I should've known better. But even before Cameron's heroic outburst, when I'd been afraid that the verdict might go this way in the end, I'd expected at least a *little* argument, some token resistance, considering every last one of us knew that the Anns were guilty as sin.

Actually, I was surprised at how mad I was. Surprised, too, by how *surprised* I was. The system was doomed from the start; the jury had been rigged since Shannon's first lie. Ivy had never stood a snowball's chance in hell.

I said, "Come on, guys, all Ivy's asking for is a stinking apology and to be left alone. What would it hurt if she got that?"

Shannon stood up and said, "Sorry, Marco. But we already voted." Then she gave me a fake sympathetic shrug, as if she would help if she could, but she just couldn't.

Everybody but me got to their feet. "We could revote," I said.

Shannon opened the heavy door and said, over her shoulder, "Is there anyone here who wants to change their vote?"

No one raised a hand or said a word.

"There ya go!" Shannon said cheerfully. "We revoted."

What could I do? My dad always said, "You do what you can, and that's all you can do." But it didn't seem like nearly enough.

As we left the custodian's closet and shuffled down the hall, no one talked. And I knew, or at least suspected, that every one of them, except Shannon and Kyle, was ashamed. Maybe they hated themselves for this. Well, that made two of us, because I hated them too.

I told you this wasn't gonna be a pretty picture.

IVY

I was trying to roll a quarter across my knuckles and weave it through my fingers when the classroom sprang a leak and the jury gushed in. Shannon led the way, smiling. The rest looked dull-eyed, as if they'd been out of the water too long. The last one, Marco, swam in looking sharklike and hungry. Was it my delicious blood he smelled?

"Have you reached a verdict?" Ms. Gold asked.

"Yep!" Shannon answered. Not *yes*, or *we have*, but *yep*. The perkiest of all possible yeses. "Five to one."

Ms. Gold clapped her tiny hands with delight. "Almost unanimous!" she cheered.

Staring hard at my quarter, I decided to flip. Heads meant the world was full of compassion and justice and I was crazy to think everyone hated me. But if it landed on tails, the world was cruel and insane and I alone was clear-sighted enough to see it.

Heads, I'm nuts; tails, everyone hates me. What lovely choices!

Ms. Gold made us drag our desks into our courtroom positions one last time. Jeremy put his jacket on backward to look like a judge's robe. Ms. Gold had Ann, Benita, and Owen stand next to Sophie's empty chair.

Daria came up beside me and squeezed my arm, making me drop my quarter. It rolled under Ms. Gold's desk and twinkled like a shiny scale. I wanted to dive for it, but Daria's cold fingers were clutching my sleeve. It was the least I could do to let her hold on to me, since she was so wobbly. But I hoped no one went for my coin before me. I kept my eye on it, just in case.

Shannon handed Jeremy a piece of paper.

Jeremy cleared his throat importantly and said, "Ms. Linda S. Gold's third-period American Government class finds the codefendants . . ." He paused there for dramatic effect, then said, "Not liable!"

The classroom exploded.

At least that's how it seemed to me. Jeremy was pounding. Owen was bellowing. Benita was shrieking. I couldn't tell if they were shrieks of joy or sorrow, but I knew that whatever Benita felt, the opposite should be true for me.

Eventually, my mind grasped that it was tails.

I ducked down to grab my quarter. On my way up, I saw Shannon lean over to say something to Ann. Whatever it was made Ann stop dead and stare a stream of angry-hate at Marco. That was strange. I always thought she *liked* him. At least it had seemed to me that the only time Ann's mean little eyes lost their hard edge was when she was looking at Marco. Not anymore, I guess.

Then I got it, and I couldn't help smiling—Marco must've been the one vote for me, against her! Ha!

But why was I wasting thought on *them* now, when everything was so awfully about *me*? Maybe because watching them was as safe and distant as watching goldfish in a bowl, while hearing that everyone but Marco thought it was okay that The Evil Three made my life a living hell was surreal. Actually, it was almost satisfyingly nightmarish. It proved it hadn't been all in my head. I hadn't *imagined* I was alone on earth—I really was alone.

Einstein whispered, "I'm so sorry, Ivy." And she looked sorry. More than sorry. She looked upset to discover that the world, or at least Sea View School, really was a nasty, unfair place. Poor Daria, I thought.

I said, "Oh, that's okay," and I practically meant it, so I added, "Don't worry about it." Then I shook my head over the irony of *me* feeling sorry for *her.*

The bell rang and everyone swam for the door, flowing into the hall, adding themselves to the surging crowd swimming away. I filled my gills, flicked my tail, and joined in once more.

BRYCE

Dude, it's like the old line says—if there was a contest for losers, Poison Ivy would come in second.

She did not win the dicer-slicer-o-matic or the all-expenses-paid weekend getaway for two. And the moral is that *winners win and losers lose*. Actually, someone told me that Poison Ivy's in the nuthouse for trying to ice herself. But who knows? She could just be home with the flu, for all I know.

On the other hand, I saw Einstein and Cam about to swap spit by the gym, so at least *they* got something outta this. And I made twenty-six potatoes, clear profit. Dude!

ANN

The trial was a *total* waste of time. As a rule, I'm all for wasting time. Still, looking around at the lame specimens in my class was so depressing. It didn't even count as a victory, they were all so *weenie*. What's a girl gotta do to get a worthy opponent around this place? I tell you, the lack of intelligence, lack of creativity, not to mention guts, well, it's enough to make you hurl.

There was Owen with his head up his butt, thinking he'd been so brilliant. And Daria, cowering with her tail between her legs like a wormy mutt at the pound. And Jeremy, forget Jeremy, he's such a weasel. And Benita was practically crying she was so . . . *what*? Relieved? Like there was ever any doubt? And then she *hugged* Owen! Eww! Talk about hurling!

And Ms. G amazed me too. Where did she get off looking shocked? Like this wasn't the way everyone always *knew* it would turn out?

And Shannon, all full of herself and her news flash that *Marco* had betrayed me. Which figures. Stings a little I admit, but figures. I'd been sweet as frosting to that boy and what'd he do? Stabbed me in the back, that's what.

I looked around the room in disgust at everyone celebrating and carrying on. But then, guess what? I noticed that the *only* person who kept her cool and wasn't acting like a complete head case was *Poison Ivy,* of all people! She stood there fiddling with a quarter, calm and bored as if she were just waiting for a bus.

That totally cracked me up. I mean it.